"Sarah, just look at yourself."

She hesitated, fear nibbling at the edge of her consciousness. She didn't want to ruin this magical, wonderful spell Jake had woven, and certainly didn't want to leave this incredible, star-strewn place he'd taken her. If she opened her eyes, it might all disappear. She wanted to cling to the fantasy a little longer. He'd made her feel like a swan. She didn't want to look in the mirror and see an ugly duckling.

"Open your eyes," he urged softly. "I want you to see how beautiful you are."

Her heart raced and tripped, and the air in her lungs felt hot and heavy. Her breath came in short, shallow puffs. Slowly, slowly she opened her eyes.

He met her gaze in the mirror. "You're beautiful," he whispered.

And suddenly she felt it. For the first time in her life, she truly felt beautiful.

Dear Reader,

This month, Silhouette Romance is celebrating the classic love story. That intensely romantic, emotional and compelling novel you just can't resist. And leading our month of classic love stories is *Wife without a Past* by Elizabeth Harbison, a deeply felt tale of an amnesiac wife who doesn't recognize the FABULOUS FATHER she'd married....

Pregnant with His Child... by bestselling author Carla Cassidy will warm your heart as a man is reunited with the child he never knew existed—and the woman he never stopped loving. Next, our MEN! promotion continues, as Silhouette Romance proves a good man isn't hard to find in *The Stranger's Surprise* by Laura Anthony. In Patricia Thayer's moving love story, *The Cowboy's Convenient Bride,* a woman turns up at a Texas ranch with a very poignant secret. And in *Plain Jane Gets Her Man* by Robin Wells, you'll be delighted by the modern-day Cinderella who wins the man of her dreams. Finally, Lisa Kaye Laurel's wonderful miniseries, ROYAL WEDDINGS, continues with *The Prince's Baby.*

As the Thanksgiving holiday approaches, I'd like to give a special thanks to all of you, the readers, for making Silhouette Romance such a popular and beloved series of books. Enjoy November's titles!

Regards,

Melissa Senate
Senior Editor
Silhouette Books

Please address questions and book requests to:
Silhouette Reader Service
U.S.: 3010 Walden Ave., P.O. Box 1325, Buffalo, NY 14269
Canadian: P.O. Box 609, Fort Erie, Ont. L2A 5X3

PLAIN JANE
GETS HER MAN

Robin Wells

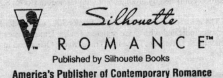

Silhouette

ROMANCE™

Published by Silhouette Books

America's Publisher of Contemporary Romance

To Ken, who fills my life with love and laughter.

With special thanks to the ladies at Care-A-Lot Childminders for sharing their knowledge and expertise.

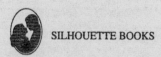 SILHOUETTE BOOKS

ISBN 0-373-19262-2

PLAIN JANE GETS HER MAN

Copyright © 1997 by Robin Rouse Wells

This edition published by arrangement with Harlequin Books S.A.

® and TM are trademarks of Harlequin Books S.A., used under license. Trademarks indicated with ® are registered in the United States Patent and Trademark Office, the Canadian Trade Marks Office and in other countries.

Printed in U.S.A.

ROBIN WELLS

Before becoming a full-time writer, Robin was a public-relations executive whose career ran the gamut from writing and producing award-winning videos to organizing pie-throwing classes taught by circus clowns. At other times in her life she has been a model, a reporter and even a charm-school teacher. But her lifelong dream was to become an author—a dream no doubt inspired by having parents who were both librarians and who passed on their love of books.

Robin lives just outside of New Orleans with her husband and two young daughters, Taylor and Arden. Although New Orleans is known as America's Most Romantic City, Robin says her personal romantic inspiration is her husband, Ken.

Robin is an active member of the Southern Louisiana chapter of the Romance Writers of America. Her first book won RWA's national 1995 Golden Heart Award.

When she's not writing, Robin enjoys gardening, antiquing, discovering new restaurants and spending time with her family.

All underlined places are fictitious.

Chapter One

"**W**here's my daddy?"

Good question, thought Sarah Anderson, pushing her tortoise shell glasses up on her nose and glancing again at the large clock on the wall. Closing time for Happy Times Preschool had come and gone a good hour ago.

"I'm sure he'll be here soon, Nikki. Would you like a snack?"

The little girl shook her head, her fine blond hair flying like dandelion fuzz. Her lower lip trembled. "I want my daddy."

Sarah knelt and put her arm around the four-year-old. It was the child's first day at the preschool, and Sarah knew it had been a long one. She searched for a way to divert her for a little while longer. "I'll bet he's on his way, honey. Why don't we make a surprise for him?"

"What kinda surprise?"

"A collage."

"What's a 'lage?"

"A picture made from other pictures. We'll find photos of things you did today, cut them out and paste them on a piece of paper. That way your dad can see what you did at school.''

Nikki regarded her thoughtfully, wavering between tears and agreement. She finally nodded. "Okay."

With a sigh of relief, Sarah rounded up the necessary supplies and settled the child in the art center. She'd just put a tape by Raffi in the cassette player and made sure Nikki knew how to safely use a pair of blunt-tipped scissors when the chimes on the front door jangled.

Sarah looked up, expecting to see the tall, muscular cowboy who had registered his little girl that morning. Instead she saw the short, portly form of Deb Kloster, her best friend and business partner.

Sarah followed her friend into the kitchen alcove, out of the child's earshot. "It's your day off. What are you doing here?"

"I was about to ask you the same question," Deb replied with a pointed glance at the clock. "I saw your car still parked out front and decided to stop in and see why you're missing the community volunteer meeting." Deb shook her gray head disapprovingly. "You'll never meet any eligible men spending all your time here, Sarah."

Sarah drew a deep breath. Deb was constantly pestering her about meeting men, and the topic was growing tiresome. She means well, Sarah reminded herself, smoothing a strand of hair away from her face and adjusting one of her two barrettes. Deb's own twenty-five-year marriage was nothing short of blissful, and she only wanted Sarah to find the same kind of happiness.

But Sarah didn't share the older woman's optimism about her chances. She had a pretty good idea of what most men were looking for in a woman, and her mirror told her she didn't have it. She'd been forced to face the truth a long time ago: she was as plain as unbuttered toast. And the fact that she usually got tongue-tied and red-faced when she tried to make a good impression didn't help matters, either. She had no more idea how to flirt than how to fly.

Besides, Oak Grove, Texas, was not exactly teeming with men who were husband material. With a population just shy of six thousand, it wasn't exactly teeming, period—especially with single men in her pushing-thirty age category.

All the same, she'd agreed to take Deb's advice and go to tonight's meeting about countywide volunteer opportunities. She didn't have any hopes of meeting Mr. Right, but she wanted to find a worthwhile activity to fill her evenings and weekends. She was always at her happiest when she was doing something useful, and the little favors she loved doing for her friends and neighbors still left her with too much time on her hands. She'd been spending most of her free time alone ever since her grandmother had died a year ago, and it was getting darn lonesome.

But her personal situation was not what concerned her now. She inclined her head toward the child in the next room. "We have a new student. Her father was supposed to pick her up at five, and he still hasn't shown up. I'm starting to get worried."

Deb's brow furrowed in a frown. "Did he leave the name and number of someone else to call in case of an emergency?"

Sarah picked up the information card the father had filled out that morning, then peered around the doorway to check on the child. The tape player was blaring a song about bubble gum, but Sarah spoke in low tones all the same. "No. He said he'd just moved to town and didn't know anyone here yet. He's a single father. He just bought the old Murphy ranch."

"You've tried his home number?"

"About a dozen times, and every time I've left a message on his machine."

"What's his name?"

"Jake Masters."

"I'll check with the county hospital, then call the police," Deb said decisively.

"No, don't call the police! They'll take the girl into custody, contact the child-welfare officials and scare the poor child to death."

"It's nearly seven-thirty. We've got to do something."

Sarah glanced at Nikki, who was cutting a picture out of a magazine, her mouth puckered in concentration. She couldn't bring herself to turn the little girl over to the authorities. She would end up being questioned and processed and shuffled around for half the night. Sarah's brow creased in worry. "Maybe the father's sick. Or hurt."

"Or guilty of serious child neglect. Maybe even abandonment."

"Oh, no! I'm certain it's nothing like that."

Deb shook her head. "You never want to believe anything bad about anyone, Sarah, but believe me, it happens. We just don't see much of it in Oak Grove."

"Thank heavens," Sarah murmured. Deb had worked in a preschool for underprivileged children in Dallas, and Sarah knew she'd seen some heartbreaking situations—situations that Sarah could hardly imagine, situations that brought tears to her eyes just to hear about.

"We don't know anything about this man," Deb continued. "We don't even know whether he really lives here or not. For that matter, we don't actually know if this child is even his daughter."

"Oh, I'm sure it's his child," Sarah insisted. "They've got exactly the same eyes. And I'm certain it was his voice on the answering machine." It was a distinctive voice— deep and low and masculine, with a just hint of a west Texas drawl.

"What does this guy look like, anyway?"

My idea of heaven. Sarah bit back the response. This was not the time to tell her friend how the man had affected her when he'd registered his daughter this morning—how his brown eyes had made her knees melt like ice cream in the summer sun, how his voice had soaked right through her skin, and how the kiss he'd planted on Nikki's cheek

as he'd said goodbye had been tender enough to bring tears
to her eyes. If she mentioned her reaction to Deb, the older
woman would start concocting matchmaking schemes.

And the rancher was definitely not her type. Not that she
had a type, Sarah mentally amended. But if she did, he
definitely wouldn't be it.

For starters, he was entirely too good-looking. In her
experience, handsome men usually had a case of arrested
character development. It probably wasn't even their fault
that they tended to be shallow and vain and superficial, she
thought; most likely it was just natural for them to value
the things that had always been valued in them.

Anyway, even if a handsome man turned out to be a
halfway-decent individual, the fact remained that good-
looking men attracted good-looking women, and Sarah
knew better than to try to compete in the looks department.
She'd discovered as a teenager that beauty was a commod-
ity, like money. The world was divided into haves and
have-nots, and she'd learned the hard way where she fell
in the spectrum. Like a house or car she couldn't afford,
there was no point in pining for someone beyond her
means.

Besides, Jake Masters had been so absorbed in his
daughter this morning that he hadn't seemed to notice her
at all, and Sarah had an ironclad rule she'd vowed never
to break: never, ever, would she allow herself to show even
the slightest bit of interest in a man who hadn't first shown
an unmistakable interest in her. Never, ever—not in a million years, not if she lived to be a thousand—would she
make a fool of herself over a man.

Never again, anyway.

"So what's he like?" Deb persisted.

Sarah gave a noncommittal shrug. "Tall. Tanned. Dark
hair. Brown eyes." She peered around the doorway to
check on the little girl again. "He really seemed to love
the child, Deb. And Nikki seems crazy about him."

"They always are, honey. Even kids with horrible parents are usually attached to them. You know that."

Deb was right, Sarah conceded. Just because Jake Masters looked nice didn't mean he was. She, of all people, should know that appearances could be deceiving.

But whether he was an ideal parent or an irresponsible lout didn't change anything. Sarah had always had a soft spot in her heart for children, but Nikki had found the marshmallow center. There was a wistfulness, a seriousness, an eagerness for affection in the little girl that Sarah found endearing, and she was determined to exhaust every alternative before she caused the child any unnecessary anguish.

"Let's give the father the benefit of the doubt," Sarah cajoled. "I'd appreciate it if you'd check with the hospital. If he's not there, maybe you can stay with the child while I drive out to the ranch."

Deb clucked disapprovingly. "You shouldn't go out there alone, Sarah. It's not safe. Why, he might be drunk or crazy or involved in some sort of illegal activity...." She shook her head. "Sometimes you're just too nice for your own good."

Deb was old enough to be her mother and to Sarah's chagrin, she sometimes acted as if she were. Sarah had endured enough mothering to last two lifetimes. "I'll be fine. Can you watch the child, or do I need to call Maureen?" Sarah asked, naming one of their assistants.

Deb sighed. "I'll stay. But I don't think it's a good idea for you to go alone. I'd send Harry, but he's in Dallas on business and won't be back until tomorrow." She paused and looked up hopefully. "Why don't you ask Will to go with you?"

Sarah grimaced. Will O'Shea was a perfectly nice man—if you liked men who were dumb as a post, annoying as a swarm of mosquitoes, and had breath like week-old tuna. He'd been pestering Sarah to go out with him ever since she'd moved to Oak Grove, and she'd done everything in her power to discourage him. Calling him now would only make him redouble his efforts.

It was a sad commentary on the state of her life that Will was the only man either one of them could think to call. Deb's get-out-there-and-mingle advice might not be so far off-base, after all. Sarah wasn't likely to meet a mate, but it sure wouldn't hurt to widen her circle of friends.

"I'll be fine," she repeated, ducking out of the kitchen to check on the child.

As Sarah approached, Nikki looked up, her eyes dark and somber. Her lashes were long enough to cast shadows on her chubby cheeks. "Do you think Daddy's gone to be with Mommy?"

Sarah's eyebrows flew up in surprise. This was one possibility that hadn't occurred to her. "Why, I don't know, honey. Where's your mommy?"

"In heaven. Daddy says she's the most bootiful angel there."

A lump formed in Sarah's throat like a ball of clay.

"Mommy was a booty queen. She had a crown and ever'thin'. Daddy says she was the prettiest girl ever."

"Then she must have looked a lot like you," Sarah said softly, meaning it. With her cherubic face, Cupid's-bow mouth and white-blond curls, Nikki looked like she belonged on the cover of a Valentine's card.

"I think you're pretty, too, Miz Sarah," she said solemnly.

Sarah knelt down and clasped the child in a tight hug, the lump in her throat growing larger. "Thank you, Nikki."

One of the wonderful things about young children was the way they confused kindness with beauty, she thought. She was fairly certain no one over the age of ten would ever call her pretty. Her face was too long, her hair was too straight and mousy, and her features all somehow just missed the mark. On the plus side, she had good teeth, her skin was smooth and clear, and her ears lay nice and flat against her head.

Hardly the assets to put her in the same league as a beauty queen, Sarah noted wryly.

"So do you think Daddy's with Mommy?" Nikki asked.

A surge of protectiveness toward the girl suddenly filled Sarah's chest, along with a flash of anger at her father. He had better have one heck of a good excuse for worrying his child like this.

She reined in her emotions and forced a smile. "I'll tell you what I think. I think your Dad will be here really soon. He probably had car trouble or some other little problem, and I'm sure he'll be here as soon as he gets it worked out." She forced a brightness into her voice that she didn't feel and gave the little girl another squeeze. "Come on— why don't you show me what you've cut out for your collage? We'll paste it together. Then I'll introduce you to my friend Deb and you can help me make some peanut-butter-and-jelly sandwiches. I'm hungry, and I'll bet you are, too."

Forty-five minutes later, Sarah turned her small hatchback onto the unpaved road that led to the Murphy ranch. Her headlights beamed on the inauspicious entrance—a simple metal frame that looked like a football goal with the old Murphy brand, a large *M* in a circle, swinging overhead.

Jake Masters wouldn't even need to change the sign, Sarah mused. She wondered if the rest of the place was as well-suited to the man as the brand. Ranching was hard work, often as unrewarding as it was backbreaking. It took a certain type of man to make a go of it: one who was persistent, strong-willed, and usually a loner. Based on his appearance, she wouldn't have pegged Jake Masters as the type. It wasn't a line of business that attracted too many men with movie-star good looks. She'd always thought men who looked like Jake usually gravitated to easier jobs— jobs that allowed them to coast through life on little more than a well-timed smile.

But it was really none of her business, she chided herself.

She was here to see if he was in any sort of trouble, not check out his aptitude for ranching.

Her tires crunched on the dry dirt as she drove slowly through the entrance, her lack of speed caused as much by her lack of a plan as much as by the rough condition of the road. Overhead, a half-moon glistened in the late-May sky. How the heck did she expect to find anything, much less anyone, at night? Her self-confidence wavered. Maybe Deb was right; maybe she was on a fool's errand, a wild-goose chase, or worse.

Her mind drifted back to the small towheaded girl she'd left asleep on a mat at the preschool, and she tightened her grip on the steering wheel, simultaneously tightening her resolve.

A large, dark house loomed into view as her car topped a hill. Not a single light shone on the porch or in any of the windows, but a pickup truck was parked in the driveway. Sarah pulled up behind it, switched off the engine, and climbed out. The sound of the slamming car door reverberated in the quiet night.

"Mr. Masters?" she called out. The rhythmic drone of tree frogs in the live oaks on the lawn was the only response she heard.

With Deb's dire warnings replaying in her mind, Sarah screwed up her courage and mounted the steps to the long wooden porch that ran the length of the two-story farmhouse and knocked. No answer.

She hesitantly tried the door, and her pulse quickened when she found it unlocked. Perhaps he'd been injured—tripped on the stairs or slipped in the shower or been hurt in some such scenario. From the first-aid training she'd taken to secure her preschool license, she knew it was a fact that most accidents happened at home.

All the same, it was hard to imagine the tall, muscular man she'd met this morning stumbling or falling. He'd looked strong and powerful and more than adequately coordinated. It was far easier to picture him stark naked, his tanned muscles gleaming in the candlelight as he swept her off her feet and carried her to a massive bed draped in black satin sheets....

Heat scorched her cheeks. *Where on earth had that thought come from?* Merciful heavens, she chided herself, clutching her throat; she must be more rattled by this whole situation than she'd realized. It was unlike her to indulge in steamy romantic fantasies, especially about someone she'd just met. Someone who was clearly out of her league. Someone who was the parent of one of her students, for Pete's sake!

She drew a deep breath, forced the disturbing image out of her mind and steeled her nerves. "Mr. Masters?" she called again, pushing the door open.

She found a light switch in the hall and flipped it on. The house was sparsely furnished and filled with partially-unpacked boxes. She moved rapidly through the lower floor of the house, checking each room, then headed upstairs.

The master bedroom contained two suitcases, a dozen unpacked boxes, a bureau, a chest of drawers, a large antique armoire and a king-size mattress on the floor. The mattress, Sarah noted with relief, was covered with plain white cotton sheeting. Not a single candle was in sight.

The last bedroom she entered made her pause just inside the doorway. Instead of boxes and bare necessities, this room was fully furnished. A low, single bed covered with a Cinderella bedspread stretched against one wall; across from it were a small bureau and a carefully-arranged play area with a child-size table and chairs. Pictures of ballerinas hung on the wall, and the shelf on the far side of the room was filled with toys, puzzles and children's books.

"Nikki's room," she murmured. Jake Masters was still living out of a suitcase himself, but he'd gotten his daughter's room all arranged.

Any man who would go to this much trouble to make his child feel at home would not deliberately abandon her, Sarah thought with conviction.

So where the heck *was* he? A sense of dread tightened her stomach. She recalled Nikki's question about whether or not her daddy had gone to join her mother, and a shiver chased through her.

If that was his truck in the drive, he must be on the property somewhere. Filled with a sense of urgency, she clattered down the stairs and back outside. The outline of a barn loomed down the road in the moonlight. She would check there, she decided, climbing into her car and pulling out of the drive so fast her tires threw gravel. If she didn't find him at the barn, she would come back and call the police to help with the search. With any luck, she would be able to convince them to let Nikki stay with her while they looked for her father.

Her headlights picked up something in the road as she neared the barn, and her heart thudded hard against her rib cage. It was a horse, she realized—its saddle askew and its reins dragging on the ground.

As she drew closer, the animal lowered its head and nudged something in the grass beside the road. Her stomach lurched sickeningly, and she somehow knew what she would find.

Dear God, she prayed, *please don't let him be dead.*

She jerked the steering wheel so that her car's headlights beamed at the ominous spot in the grass, then slammed on her brakes and opened her door. The animal whinnied and backed away. Her legs felt like rubber as she hurried out of the car.

"Mr. Masters?" His name came out as a hoarse whisper. She forced herself to walk forward.

Sure enough, a man lay sprawled on the grass, next to a large outcropping of rocks. He was perfectly still, his handsome face pale and lifeless in the glare of the headlights. She reached out a trembling hand to check for a pulse, nearly jumping out of her skin when he gave a low groan.

Thank goodness! He was alive!

"Mr. Masters, can you hear me?" She placed a palm

against his face. He moved his head, moaned and opened his eyes.

"Where…what…who…?" he croaked.

His initial impression was of a beam of light and a pair of the softest, kindest eyes he'd ever seen. For a moment, he thought he was looking at an angel.

But if he were dead, his head wouldn't feel like it was about to explode, would it? Besides, he didn't think angels wore tortoise shell glasses and matching barrettes.

He tried to raise himself up, then fell back with a groan. "My head," he rasped.

"Does anything else hurt?"

Everything hurt. "My leg. My shoulder."

"Can you move them?"

He shifted his limbs experimentally. If only the pain in his head would let up for a moment. His thoughts were fractured and scattered, and he tried to rope them together into some kind of coherent memory. A single thought crystallized with sudden clarity. "Nikki." He struggled to sit up. He clutched his head, groaned again and sank back down.

"She's fine," the woman reassured him. "Let me look at your head."

"Where is she? Who are you?"

"I'm Sarah Anderson, Nikki's preschool teacher. We met this morning—remember? She's at school with my partner." Her hands were gentle on his scalp. All the same, he winced as she touched a spot that felt like it had been seared with a branding iron. "You've got a nasty cut and a huge bump." Her hands moved down his head, gently smoothing his hair.

The sympathetic gesture made him feel strangely calm and soothed. He gazed up at her, and the warmth in her eyes spread to his chest. Was she real or a figment of his imagination?

He wasn't accustomed to such tender treatment. He distinctly remembered his stepmother's irritation when he'd broken his arm at the age of ten and she'd had to cancel her bridge party. And his wife's reaction to anyone's injuries or ailments had been even less sympathetic. He'd never forget how annoyed she'd been the first time Nikki was sick.

Jake closed his eyes, wanting to shut out that vivid memory.

Funny, but his more recent memories weren't nearly as clear. He opened his lids and stared at Sarah. His vision was blurred by the throbbing in his head, and he struggled to recall meeting her that morning. She had asked him to fill out some paperwork, then focused all of her attention on his child. He remembered liking the way she'd put Nikki at ease, but otherwise, he couldn't recall much about her.

It seemed like she'd been rather nondescript. Was this the same woman? He didn't know how he ever could have thought someone with eyes like hers was nondescript.

"Your shoulder's bleeding. Let me take a look."

Cool fingers swiftly undid the buttons on the front of his denim shirt. He heard her give a sharp intake of breath.

He gritted his teeth, prepared for bad news. "How bad is it?"

"The...the cut looks superficial, but you've got a bad bruise." Her voice was slightly breathless, and her eyes refused to make contact with his. Jake didn't know whether to believe her or not.

She moved around him, and he felt her hands low on his right leg. He leaned up on his elbow and watched her examine his calf. "It looks like you're cut. Your jeans are already ripped, but I need to tear them a little more to see what we're dealing with." He clenched his teeth as she tugged. A loud rip rent the air.

Her brows knit together above her glasses. "You're going to need some stitches. If you can take off your shirt, I'll use it to wrap your leg to slow the bleeding. Then we need to get you to the hospital."

"Got to get Nikki," Jake muttered. "She'll be worried."

"She was asleep when I left," she said. "She's in good hands. My partner has thirty years' experience with children." Her face hovered above him. "Can you sit up?"

With a tremendous effort, he managed to oblige. Cool night air hit his chest as she slid off his shirt.

He watched her fold it until it was the same width as the sleeves, then slip it under his leg. He bit his lip against the pain as she tightly tied it around his wound.

She studied him worriedly. "Do you think you can make it to your feet? If you can, lean on me and I'll help you to the car."

It went against Jake's grain to lean on anybody, much less a woman. Most of the women he'd known would prop a man up just to watch him fall over.

She mistook his hesitation for doubt. "Maybe I should go call an ambulance. It'll take it about half an hour to get here from town, but—"

"I can make it," he interrupted curtly.

"I'll move my car closer."

She hurried to the vehicle and started the engine. The headlights grew blindingly brighter, then stopped a few feet from where he sat propped on the ground. He closed his eyes against the harsh glare.

He heard the car door slam, then felt her beside him again. "Ready?" she asked.

He gave a grunt and hauled himself to his feet. The pain in his leg made his knees start to buckle, but before they did, she draped his arm around her shoulder and placed an arm around his waist.

She was tall, maybe five feet seven inches, but she felt slight against him—so thin he could feel the bones in her shoulder under his arm. Despite her lack of bulk, she was strong. She was somehow managing to move his six-foot-two frame toward her vehicle.

He drew a deep breath, trying to steel himself against the pain ricocheting through his body, and caught a whiff of the soft, herbal scent of her hair. It brushed his cheek, the silky strands snagging on the stubble of his five o'clock shadow. It occurred to him that he hadn't felt a woman's hair against his face in years. Hadn't felt a woman this close to him, hadn't felt female arms around him, hadn't inhaled a woman's scent...

Her arm shifted, and the warm softness against his side was replaced by cold, hard metal. Mercy, he must be more out of it than he'd realized, he thought groggily. She'd propped him against the car like a sack of oats while she opened the door.

Judging by the direction his thoughts had been taking, he'd evidently knocked a few screws loose in that fall. He'd made up his mind after Clarissa that he was through with women. Having struck out once, he wasn't a big enough fool to go another round.

He shook his head, trying to clear it. The motion only succeeded in worsening the throbbing there, and he leaned his cheek against the cool metal of the car roof.

No, sirree, he reminded himself, *Nikki wouldn't be put through that.* Every relationship ended sooner or later, and it was always ugly when it did. Thank heavens, Nikki had been too young to know what was going on with his marriage—and too young to remember anything now.

Some people just weren't cut out for love and marriage, and he'd accepted the fact that he was one of them. He was probably genetically programmed for failure. After all, his father's luck with women had been even worse than his.

"Here we go," Sarah said, easing him onto the seat. He leaned back against the vinyl headrest, exhausted by the effort of moving. He was so tired, so sleepy.

For a moment he thought he was floating, then he realized she was lifting his feet and placing them inside the car. He hadn't even been aware they were still draped out the door. Jiminy, he was feeble as a newborn kitten. As groggy as he was, he was alert enough to know he didn't like it—not one bit. He didn't like relying on anyone for anything. Especially not a woman. Especially not one who smelled and felt as good as this one, who had eyes like an angel, and who stirred up thoughts and feelings he wanted to forget.

He tried to rouse himself as she circled the vehicle and seated herself in the driver's seat, wanting to act alert and in charge. "Thanks for your trouble." Was it his imagination, or was he slurring his words? His tongue felt thick and heavy. "If you'll just give me a ride to your school, I'll get my girl and go."

His vision was blurred, but it seemed like her eyes held an unnecessary amount of amusement. "You've got to take care of yourself before you'll be able to take care of your daughter." She started the engine. "We're going straight to the hospital."

He couldn't form the words to mount a protest.

"Nikki is just fine," she softly reassured him.

Clinging to that thought, he closed his eyes and mercifully sank into a deep, dark place that the pain couldn't reach.

At the county hospital's emergency room, a gray-haired doctor began to examine Jake's head.

Sarah edged toward the door. "I'll wait outside."

The doctor glanced up briefly. "No need to leave. I'll want to ask you a few questions when I finish examining him."

"But...but..."

The doctor peered over his glasses and grinned. "I promise not to remove any more of his clothes without giving you fair warning."

Thank goodness. Sarah swallowed and gave a weak smile. From the moment she'd unbuttoned Jake's shirt to check his shoulder, she'd been unable to keep her eyes away from the wide expanse of tanned, naked man, unable to stop her pulse from skittering and skipping every time she got a look at the muscled slope of his chest and the taut, rippled plane of his belly.

It was not a sight she was used to seeing—not up close, at any rate. She'd seen her ex-fiancé's chest, of course, but Dave's body hadn't affected her anything like this.

But then, it hadn't looked anything like this, either, Sarah realized. Dave's body had been scrawny and pale. It hadn't made her feel fevered and chilled at the same time, hadn't made her imagine how it would feel to run her hands over it—hadn't made her wonder how its warm weight would feel on top of her as she was wondering now.

Her face burning, Sarah lowered herself onto a vinyl chair in the far corner of the room and twisted her fingers in her lap.

"What happened?" the doctor asked, beaming a penlight in Jake's eyes.

"Stupid accident," Jake muttered. "A snake spooked my horse, and I got thrown."

The word "snake" raised the hair on Sarah's neck. Just the thought of the creatures was enough to make her skin crawl. She couldn't stand the slithery beasts. In her mind, they were indelibly associated with pain and humiliation and...

A tremor seized her, and panic rose in her throat. *Don't think about it,* she ordered herself, forcing her thoughts back to the present.

"Did you get bitten?" the doctor was asking Jake.

"Naw. Looked like a garter snake."

"We'll check you over thoroughly just to be sure."

Sarah found her gaze again riveted on Jake's chest. She swallowed hard and averted her eyes, only to find them drawn back again. Jake's pectorals were just the thing to keep her thoughts off all things cold-blooded; the sight of his naked flesh made her blood simmer in her veins.

Her eyes traced the dark line of crisp hair down his belly to the spot below his navel where it disappeared into his jeans. Mesmerized, she watched as the doctor pushed and prodded the hard, horizontal muscles of his stomach as he checked for internal injuries.

"You say he fell asleep in the car on the way to the hospital?"

Sarah started, surprised to find that the doctor had turned away from Jake and was addressing her directly. "Y-yes."

The doctor pushed his glasses up on his nose. "Well, I'd say he's probably got a mild concussion. We'll do a CT scan to be sure. And his leg is going to need sewing up. We'll x-ray the shoulder, but I don't think anything's broken. Most probably he'll need to stay in the hospital for a few days, then take it easy at home for a couple of weeks after that."

Jake raised himself on an elbow, his expression alarmed. "I can't do that, Doc. I've got a four-year-old daughter and a ranch to run."

"I'm afraid you've got no choice. You're pretty well banged up. Your head will probably be fine in a couple of days, but we need to keep an eye on you until it's better. After that, you'll need to stay off that leg, and with your shoulder in that condition, you're not going to be able to get around very well on crutches."

Keeping up with a preschooler was hard work for a normal, healthy adult, Sarah thought sympathetically. How would he manage with all his injuries? "Do you have any family or friends you want me to call?" she asked.

Jake sank back heavily on the examining table. "No one who can look after Nikki. She has a maternal grandmother, but she's in Europe. And I don't have any family. Don't have any friends here, either. Just moved from Amarillo." He closed his eyes, as if the sheer effort of talking exhausted him. "I took out an ad for a housekeeper in the *Oak Grove Weekly,* but it won't run till next week."

The doctor frowned and rubbed his jaw. "Well, I can give you the name of some agencies in Dallas, and you can arrange for a private nurse. I think they do child care, too. It'll be mighty expensive, though, and you never know what you're likely to get. I've had some patients who've been less than happy with the help. If I were you, I'd try to hire someone locally."

"Any suggestions?"

The doctor shook his head.

Sarah instantly stepped forward. "I'll watch Nikki while you're in the hospital."

Jake drew in a long breath and gazed at her. He was already beholden to this woman, and he didn't like being indebted to anyone. On the other hand, she was a licensed child-care professional, which was more than he was likely to find through an agency.

Besides, she wouldn't be a stranger to Nikki. The poor kid hadn't even had time to adjust to the move yet, Jake thought with a stab of guilt, and now she was going to have to deal with another upheaval.

He heavily sighed. As much as he disliked the idea of accepting favors, he knew he should take Sarah up on her offer—for Nikki's sake. But he wouldn't take charity; he would insist on making this a business arrangement.

He swallowed hard and nodded. The motion made his head throb in double time. "Thanks." Even to his ears, his voice sounded gravelly. "I'll pay you well for your trouble."

"We can discuss all that later. For right now, just rest easy and know that Nikki's in good hands."

Her words didn't sound like a boast, just a statement of fact. Jake found it oddly reassuring.

"What do I need to do to take care of things at the ranch?" she asked.

The ranch. His thoughts all seemed to be wrapped in cotton—fuzzy and soft and shapeless. He grappled with one and finally managed to unswaddle it. "I—I hired a couple of ranch hands this morning. Names and numbers are in my pocket. Could you call them, ask them to take care of things for a few days? They used to work for old man Murphy, so they're familiar with the place."

"I'll be glad to." Her gray eyes grew reflective. "You

know, this whole situation will probably be easier on Nikki
if we stay at your place instead of mine. That way she'll
at least be at home.''

Jake started to nod again, then thought better of it.
"Whatever you think is best. The house is a mess, but
Nikki's room is set up.''

The doctor eyed Sarah speculatively. "If you can talk
this young lady into staying for a couple of weeks after
you're discharged from the hospital, maybe you can kill
two birds with one stone,'' he ventured. "You'll need
someone to cook for you, help you get back on your feet.''

It was Sarah's turn to hesitate. It was one thing to watch
a child, and quite another to tend to the needs of a full-
grown man. Especially a man who disconcerted her so—
who made her think outrageous thoughts, who caused her
to feel cold and hot and shivery all at the same time. Especially now, lying there shirtless.

But he has no one, Sarah realized with a sharp pang of
sympathy. She knew what it was like to be alone—to feel
friendless and lonesome and lost in the shuffle. It was how
she'd felt throughout all of high school and most of college.
Everyone else had had dates and parties and busy weekend
plans, and she'd had nothing but an awkward, debilitating
shyness. Except for the hours when she was working at the
preschool, it was pretty much how she'd been feeling
lately—how she'd felt ever since her grandmother had died.

Surely she could help this poor man out, she told herself.
He needed her, and she'd never been able to walk away
from a person in need. What could be the harm in it? After
all, a sick man was just as helpless as a child.

She glanced at him, finding her mouth suddenly dry.
Nothing about Jake Masters looked helpless. Just the opposite, in fact. He looked strong and virile and vital
and...dangerous.

Nonsense, she scolded herself. In order to be dangerous,
he would first have to be interested in her, and there was
about as much chance of that as of her being crowned Miss

America. Any man who looked like him probably went through gorgeous women as fast as Nikki could go through a bag of candy.

She was being foolish. She'd already offered to help with Nikki, and the best thing she could do for the girl was to help her father get back on his feet. Heck, she'd been looking for a constructive way to fill her free time, anyway. And Deb had been after her to take some vacation leave. The only reason she hadn't done so was because she hadn't wanted to end up with even more time on her hands.

Her mind raced as she considered the logistics. Enrollment was light during the summer session; she could easily take a week or two off, then teach half-days if Jake still wasn't over the worst of it....

"My schedule is pretty flexible," Sarah found herself saying. "I'll be happy to help out however I can."

It was the decent thing to do, she thought, trying to override the doubts fluttering in her stomach. If she were in his position, she would want someone to do the same for her.

She was simply trying to help Nikki, that was all, she told herself firmly. Her decision had nothing, absolutely nothing, to do with the way her insides quivered like a bowl of gelatin whenever Jake Masters turned his mocha-colored eyes in her direction.

Chapter Two

"Can I ride in the wheelchair with you, Daddy?"

Jake fondly eyed his daughter as she bounced beside him on the edge of his hospital bed. "As far as I'm concerned, pumpkin, you can ride in it all by yourself. I don't know why they brought the blasted contraption up here in the first place."

"Hospital regulations, Mr. Masters," said the stout, multi-chinned nurse who'd just wheeled the chair into the room. "All of our discharged patients are required to ride to the exit. Besides, you'd have a mighty hard time making it to the door with your leg in that shape."

Jake steadied himself on the metal railing as he rose from the side of the bed. His calf throbbed, his shoulder ached and his head hurt every time he moved. The wheelchair was probably a better idea than he wanted to admit. Even though three days had passed since the accident, it was still darn hard to get around.

All the same, it felt great to be up—and dressed. He would rather ride bareback in sandpaper underwear than spend another day in that ridiculous scrap of fabric they passed off as a hospital gown.

He glanced at Sarah, who was perched on a chair in the corner of the tiny room. It had been thoughtful of her to bring him a change of clothes for the trip home. But then, she'd done lots of thoughtful things during the past three days, he reflected—brought his shaving kit, collected his mail, taken him the newspaper…

And done a jam-up job taking care of Nikki. She'd brought his daughter for daily visits, and he'd been impressed with her quiet, gentle way with the child. He'd been impressed, too, with how she'd turned the situation into a learning experience for Nikki, taking time to answer her questions and explain the workings of the hospital. Thanks to Sarah, Nikki had viewed his hospital stay as a grand adventure instead of a traumatic event.

Which sure took a load off his mind. He'd been worried about how she would handle being separated from him. Judging from Nikki's happy, animated behavior, however, she'd taken their time apart a whole lot better than he had.

The nurse motioned him toward the wheelchair, then glanced at Nikki, who'd jumped off the bed and stood poised to climb into his lap the moment he sat down. "I'm afraid the rules say you have to ride alone, Mr. Masters. Your daughter will have to walk with your wife."

Wife. The word hit Jake like a slap in the face. He tensed and froze beside the chair. "I don't have a wife."

"Oh. I'm sorry. I thought…" The nurse's gaze darted to Sarah, then back to Jake. "Sorry."

The nurse was looking at him strangely. Too late, Jake realized his forehead was creased in a scowl, his hands knotted into fists at his sides. Jeezum Pete, the poor woman probably thought he was going to deck her. He sheepishly lowered himself into the wheelchair and risked a glance at Sarah.

Oh, criminy. Her reaction was even worse than the nurse's. Her face was as red as a tomato and her fingers were nervously twisting her purse strap like a strand of spaghetti on a fork.

"Miz Sarah's not my mommy," Nikki volunteered. "Mommy's in heaven. Miz Sarah's my teacher, an' she's Daddy's friend. An' she's gonna come live with us. Right, Daddy?"

"That's right," Jake said, forcing a lightness into his voice he didn't feel. He risked another glance at Sarah, wondering how she was taking Nikki's pronouncement, wondering if she was worried the nurse might think there was more to their relationship than friendship.

Sarah looked down at Nikki, and her brown hair swung forward, hiding her face. He could see that her neck was scarlet above her white T-shirt and denim jumper. The sight softened something inside him.

He didn't know when he'd last seen a full-grown woman blush. Heck, he wasn't sure he'd even known that full-grown women were capable of blushing. Most of the ones he ran across seemed to be shameless. It bothered him that he'd somehow embarrassed her, but he didn't have a clue what to do about it.

He was glad that Nikki's busy chatter filled the silence between them as they rode down in the elevator.

"I'll bring the car around to the entrance," Sarah said when the doors opened on the first floor. "Nikki, do you want to come with me or wait here with your dad?"

"Come with you!" She grabbed Sarah's hand, then hesitated and glanced at her father as the nurse wheeled him toward the entrance. "Okay, Daddy?"

"Sure," Jake said gruffly. He watched them head out the door, Nikki skipping along beside Sarah, their hands entwined, and felt an unaccustomed stab of jealousy.

He was immediately ashamed of the sentiment. He ought to be grateful Nikki got along so well with Sarah, he thought guiltily—after all, she was her preschool teacher. It was only natural that the child would have grown fond of her; Sarah had been taking care of her around the clock for the past few days.

And he *was* grateful—mighty grateful, he told himself. Sarah had been a godsend, and he didn't know what he would have done without her. He just wasn't used to sharing his daughter's affections, that was all. Nikki's babysitter back in Amarillo had been capable and competent, but Nikki had never exhibited any real attachment to her.

The nurse pushed his chair out the entrance, and he drew his first breath of fresh air in three days. He scanned the parking lot and spotted Sarah and Nikki, still hand in hand, making their way toward a small white car. He had to admit that it agreed with Nikki's taste in baby-sitters. Sarah was sure a lot more appealing than the old battle-ax they'd left behind in west Texas.

A whole lot more appealing, he thought as a gust of wind blew her skirt against her legs, outlining a surprisingly shapely backside. A surge of attraction rippled through him like the breeze in his hair, and his hands tightened on the wheelchair arms.

Whoa, there, pardner, he told himself sternly. What had gotten into him, letting his thoughts veer off in that direction? He'd managed to rein in those impulses after Clarissa's death, and life had definitely been more serene as a result. He fully intended to keep it that way.

There was something about this woman, though, that heated his blood and stirred his imagination. It was hard to say exactly what it was. She wasn't beautiful in the classic sense, but there was something about her—some indefinable, intangible thing—that made it hard for him to keep his eyes off her whenever she was around and his thoughts off her whenever she wasn't.

Presence—that was it. Sarah had presence.

Well, he'd better try to get some presence himself: the presence of mind to keep the heck away from her. The last thing he ever intended to do again was get involved with another woman.

Sarah felt Jake's eyes on her as she unlocked the car door and helped Nikki into the backseat, and she couldn't keep from glancing around after she'd adjusted the child's seat belt. Sure enough, he was watching her, a dark frown etched on his face.

Sarah stiffened. He'd worn the same displeased expression when the nurse had mistaken her for his wife. Was he insulted that the nurse had thought he was married to someone so plain and unattractive?

She was being ridiculous, she told herself as she rounded the car. Jake probably hadn't noticed her one way or the other. Just because she was unnaturally preoccupied with him didn't mean he'd given her a second thought. More than likely the poor man was still grieving for his wife, and the mention of her had struck a raw nerve, that was all.

She needed to get a grip on her overactive imagination, Sarah scolded herself, opening the door and sliding behind the steering wheel. She'd spent entirely too much time thinking about this man and finding things to like about him—the quiet way he'd thanked her for every little favor, how his eyes lit up when he saw his daughter, the way the laugh lines beside his eyes fanned out whenever he smiled....

Stop it, Sarah ordered herself as she inserted the key in the ignition. Nothing Jake had done or said implied that he had any interest in her at all except as Nikki's teacher and temporary caregiver. Oh, there had been a time or two when she thought she'd caught him looking at her, but that didn't necessarily mean anything. For all she knew, she might have had spinach stuck between her teeth. Every indication was that Jake's attention was focused solely on his child, and that was where she needed to keep hers focused, too.

Resolved to do just that, Sarah drove around to the hospital entrance, leaned across the seat, and opened the passenger door. The next thing she knew, Jake had climbed in beside her.

The interior of her car suddenly seemed much smaller and warmer, and Sarah's palms grew damp on the steering wheel as she pulled away from the curb. The faint, clean scent of his shaving cream wafted toward her, and a curl of attraction unfurled in her belly despite her resolve.

She was glad for the nonstop chatter of the talkative child in the backseat. After a Dalmation sighting and an offer to share a soggy stick of bubblegum, Nikki began a rundown of her nightly routine with Sarah.

"An' after she brushes my hair and reads me a book, Miz Sarah tells the bestest bedtime story ever—about two princesses," Nikki babbled. "Maybe she'll tell it to you tonight, too, Daddy."

Sarah felt a blush coming on as Jake shot her an amused glance.

"An' she lets me use her tape player. See?" In the rearview mirror, Sarah saw Nikki pass the small cassette player to her father. "It's got a headset an' everything. I can follow along in a picture book an' turn the pages when the bell sounds. I brought *Jack an' the Beanstalk.* Do you think you could turn it on for me, Daddy?"

Jake fiddled with the machine, then passed it back to his daughter. She clamped the earphones on her head and settled back contentedly, the book on her lap.

"That tape player's a great idea," Jake remarked. "How much quiet time will it buy us?"

Sarah grinned. "About half an hour. Long enough to get you home." She glanced at him, her eyes concerned. "How are you feeling?"

"Pretty good," he lied. The late-May sunshine hurt his eyes, and the motion of the vehicle was making his leg throb again. "It's good to be out of the hospital." That much, at least, was the truth.

He leaned back against the headrest and stared out the windshield at the unfamiliar scenery. He had no memory of arriving at the hospital, and he was still too new to town to recognize any landmarks. It made him uneasy to realize he had no idea where he was or even in which direction he was traveling. Jake made a point of always knowing exactly where he was headed.

Sarah looked like a woman who always knew where she was going, too, he thought, studying her profile. She had a strong face—a face with character. Her features might not fit the usual cookie-cutter standards of beauty, but her high, pronounced cheekbones and wide, full-lipped mouth somehow balanced everything out.

Besides, there was more to her face than the sum total of her features. When she looked straight at him, he found it hard to breathe.

It was her eyes, he realized. Large, blue-gray and expressive, they somehow softened up the rest of her face. Those eyes were as warm and soft and inviting as a feather bed. And somehow just as full of possibilities, too. The way her glasses shielded them was almost erotic—sort of like a see-through negligee for her eyes.

She turned them on him unexpectedly, and he felt a little shock wave of attraction race through him. Realizing he was staring, he glanced away and cleared his throat. "Thanks for everything you've done," he managed to say. "If it weren't for you, I might still be lying in that cow pasture."

Her laugh was warm and throaty. "I doubt that would be the case."

Her voice was nearly as special as her eyes—low and rich and a little breathy. He gazed at her, trying to figure out why it seemed so hard to separate how she sounded from how she looked. "Well, I appreciate all your help. Especially with Nikki."

"She's a wonderful child."

"Yeah. She is, isn't she?" He couldn't keep the pride from spilling into his voice.

Sarah nodded. "She's delightful—bright, inquisitive, affectionate. You've done a wonderful job."

Jake swallowed around a lump in his throat. Doing a

good job as Nikki's father was the most important thing in the world to him, and it meant a lot to have a child-care authority give him a passing grade. "Thanks."

"It must be hard being a single parent," Sarah said, glancing at him from the corner of her eye. "Was Nikki very young when her mother died?"

"Not quite two."

"That must have been awful for you." Her voice was full of sympathy. "What happened?"

"Small plane crash." Jake uneasily shifted his weight on the seat and stared out the window, his stomach tightening as it always did whenever the subject came up. He groped for a new topic and grabbed the first one that came to mind. "Have you lived in Oak Grove all your life?"

She gave a small smile, and he knew she could tell he was deliberately changing the subject. He was glad she had the grace to go along with it. "No. Just the past two years."

"Where are you from?"

"Oh, a little bit of everywhere. My dad was with an oil company, and we moved around a lot when I was growing up. I went to college in Oklahoma, then taught kindergarten there before I moved here." She took her eyes from the road and glanced at him. "What about you? Did you grow up around Amarillo?"

"Amarillo and Dallas," he replied. "My parents divorced when I was eight, and I was shuffled back and forth between them until I was twelve."

"What happened when you were twelve?"

"My mother died."

"How terrible!" She looked at him again, her eyes wide and compassionate. He felt like he could bathe in the warmth of those eyes, just soak in them until he drowned.

"So you were raised by a single father, just like Nikki."

"I wasn't that lucky. Dad remarried a year later."

Sarah darted a questioning glance at him. "Sounds like you didn't get along with your stepmother."

"Let's just say she managed to live up to all the bad

press stepmothers get in those fairy tales. And she didn't make Dad happy, either.''

''Where are they now?''

''Dad died while I was in college. She sent me a card a year later to let me know she'd married a banker in Houston.''

Jake searched for a way to change the topic back to Sarah. He wanted to learn more about this woman who'd been living at his home and watching his child. A woman who had been preying on his mind more than he wanted to admit while he'd been laid up in that hospital bed. ''So what brought you to Oak Grove?''

''My grandmother. She'd lived here all her life, then got too ill to live alone. My parents wanted her to sell her house and move to a rest home near their retirement place in Florida, but she didn't want to leave her home. She and I had always been close, so I moved down here to take care of her.'' Sarah stopped at one of the town's three traffic lights. ''She died a year ago.''

''Sorry to hear it.''

''I'm sorry about your loss, too,'' she said softly.

Jake nodded and jerked his head back toward the window. He didn't want to talk about Clarissa, and he didn't want people to feel sorry for him. Those were the main reasons he'd made this move: to make a fresh start, to avoid the pitying glances, and to keep Nikki from hearing the rumors and gossip.

The light changed, and Sarah pulled away from the intersection. ''So what brings you and Nikki to Oak Grove?''

He gave a shrug. ''My neighbor made an offer on my ranch that was too good to pass up. I figured a change might do us good. When I saw an ad for the Murphy place in a ranching magazine, I came out, took a look, and, well...here we are.''

Sarah nodded. ''I understand about needing a change. I've been living in my grandmother's house, but lately I've been thinking about selling it. It has too many memories.

Most of them are good, but still..." She gave a small sigh. "It can be kind of emotionally exhausting, getting hit with a memory every time you open the door. Sometimes I wish I lived in a place that just sat there and left me alone."

Jake laughed. She'd described exactly how he'd felt about the old ranch. It was funny, he thought; he usually didn't relate very well to people. He seemed to have better luck with animals. But Sarah and he seemed tethered to the same tree.

He glanced at her, his eyes resting on her lips, and wondered what they would feel like on his. Attraction, warm and strong, tugged at his belly, and another question formed in his mind: would they get along this well together in bed?

In bed? Jake rubbed his jaw and frowned. What the heck was the matter with him? He must have knocked all the sense out of his head when he'd hit that rock, he thought irritably. Or maybe this was the result of lying around with too much time on his hands.

Whatever the cause, he needed to corral his thoughts, and he needed to do it fast. His best bet was to corral the whole darn relationship. It was high time he put things between them into a businesslike context.

"We haven't discussed your salary yet," he said abruptly.

She glanced up, surprised. "You don't need to pay me. I'm glad I can help out."

"Nonsense." His tone was brusque, almost harsh. "You're in the child-care business, and that's what you've been doing—taking care of Nikki. Now, with me home, you'll have even more responsibilties. Of course I'm going to pay you."

"It's not necessary."

"It is to me."

Sarah heard the determination in his voice and from the corner of her eye, she saw it in his face, too. His mouth was taut, his jaw clenched, his eyes narrowed.

She was accustomed to helping people out just because

it was the neighborly thing to do, with no thought of re-muneration. But if it was going to make him uncomfortable, she would take the darn money. "All right. If you insist."

His face muscles relaxed, but his voice still held a brisk, businesslike edge. "I do. Now, as to the terms... From what the doctor said, you'll need to stay for a couple of weeks. Hopefully I'll have located a permanent housekeeper by then." He named a weekly figure that made Sarah's mouth fall open. "How does that sound?"

"Like way too much money." From the corner of her eye, she saw the beginnings of a scowl gather on his face like a storm cloud. Wanting to forestall it, she added quickly, "It's very generous. Thank you."

He gave a curt nod.

Puzzled and deflated, she turned her attention back to the road, pondering the sudden change in his manner. It was as if the whole balance of power had shifted. Instead of being friends and equals, they'd just become employee and employer. One minute he'd been talking and laughing and acting genuinely interested in her, and the next he was scowling and treating her as nothing more than hired help. One moment his attitude had been warm and friendly; the next it was cold, distant, impersonal.

She didn't know what had happened to make him change so abruptly, and she didn't know why it bothered her so. Why should she suddenly feel so let down and disap-pointed?

She knew better than to expect a relationship with a cap-ital *R* with a man like Jake, she reminded herself, guiding the car through the outskirts of town. She was asking for double-bypass heartache to even hope for it. Heck, he prob-ably had half the women in Texas beating a path to his door and knocking on it in their nighties, holding engraved invitations for him to have his way with them morning, noon, or night.

Besides, he was obviously still head over heels in love with his late wife. He couldn't even bring himself to talk about her. And while she had to admit that the ability to form a strong, enduring bond with a woman was one of the sexiest traits a man could possess, in this case, the man in question might as well be waving red flags in each hand and have a flashing light on his forehead that read "Danger".

Sarah frowned as she steered the car onto the two-lane highway. She'd always been sensible in these matters. She'd always prided herself on her ability to look at things rationally, evaluate a situation objectively, and proceed with caution.

So why was it, she wondered as she mashed her foot to the accelerator, that she had a sudden desire to throw caution to the wind?

Chapter Three

Jake awakened to a soft rapping sound. He blinked in confusion and wondered where he was, then recognized his old oak armoire against the wall. His new house. Sarah had brought him home from the hospital. He'd met briefly with his ranch hands, and then, exhausted, he'd climbed the stairs to take a brief nap.

He groped for the alarm clock on the nightstand. Six-thirty. In the morning or at night? The dim light filtering through the window shades didn't give him much of a clue.

The tapping sounded again. "Come in," he called.

The door creaked open and there stood Sarah, backlit by the hallway light. Something about the way the light glowed behind her reminded him of how she'd looked when he'd first opened his eyes after the accident—how he'd wondered if she were an angel.

She was sure turning out to be one to Nikki and him, he thought. He pushed himself up against the headboard, ran a hand through his hair and caught a whiff of something delicious. Judging from the aroma wafting from the tray in her hands, he thought, she was evidently an angel of mercy for his stomach, too.

And you're paying her well to do it, he reminded himself. *Don't go getting all mushy over it.*

Sarah nudged the door all the way open with her elbow. "I brought you dinner."

Dinner. That meant he'd slept all afternoon. "Thanks." Jake glanced at the plate of fried chicken, mashed potatoes, green beans and salad, and inhaled appreciatively. "This looks great. But you didn't have to bring it up. I could have come downstairs."

Sarah carefully set the bed tray over his lap. Her arm brushed his chest, and the contact suddenly changed everything—the temperature in the room, his ability to fill his lungs with air, his capacity to think. He had an irrational impulse to reach out and pull her down on the bed beside him.

"The doctor said for you to take it easy," she said. "I'm here to make sure you follow doctor's orders."

He flashed a grin. "How am I doing so far?"

She laughed, and the sound did something funny to his insides. So did the fact that she was here in his bedroom, standing so close he could smell the soft scent of her perfume.

He scowled at his reaction to her. An attraction to this woman was the last thing he needed right now. He had to keep his distance, he reminded himself. "I'd have to be comatose to take it any easier," he said gruffly. "It makes no sense to me that a bump on the head and a cut on my leg should make me feel this tired."

She gave a sympathetic smile. "You'll be up and around before you know it."

"Better be. I've got a lot of work to do to make this place turn a profit." He picked up a fork and turned his attention to the mashed potatoes, hoping she would take a hint and leave. But one taste made him forget his resolve.

"Mmm. This beats the heck out of the food at the hospital."

Sarah smiled again, and Jake found himself staring at her, trying to figure out how such a simple change of expression could completely transform her face. With an effort, he turned his attention back to the plate. "What's Nikki up to?"

"Playing zoo with her stuffed animals. She's dividing them by species and making cages with her Tinkertoys."

Jake grinned, mentally picturing the scene. "She started that after we visited the zoo in Dallas. No telling what she'll do if I take her to Six Flags Over Texas. Probably turn her bed into a roller coaster."

Sarah laughed in that rich, warm way she had, and Jake found himself thinking that Sarah could probably turn his bed into a roller coaster pretty easily.

"I wanted to talk to you about her schedule," she said. "If it's all right with you, I'd like her to go to school in the morning. I think she needs to stay on a regular routine."

Jake nodded, his mouth full of chicken.

"My partner, Deb, can give her a ride to and from school."

"Fine."

An awkward silence stretched between them. She moved toward the door. "Well, I'll let you eat in peace."

As unwise as he knew it was, he hated to see her go. He swept his hand around the room, indicating the neatly arranged furniture. "I, uh, appreciate everything you've done to the place. The room looks great."

"Oh." She looked around. "I probably didn't put everything exactly where you want it, but I figured it would be easier for you to change things around later than to continue living out of suitcases and boxes."

"Doesn't look like I'll need to change a thing. How'd you get the bed frame together?"

"I found a toolbox in the garage."

"You did it yourself?"

Sarah nodded.

"You've got all kinds of hidden talents." And he could think of a few he would like to explore, he mused, eyeing the buttons that ran the length of her denim jumper and imagining what lay behind each one. *Stop it, Masters,* he immediately ordered himself, but his imagination seemed stuck in overdrive.

Sarah shrugged. "When you've lived alone as long I have, you learn to do lots of things yourself."

"You've never been married?" The question was out before he had time to consider the wisdom of asking it.

"No. But I came close."

"Oh, yeah? What happened?"

Sarah shrugged. "My grandmother's illness didn't fit his five-year plan."

Jake leaned back on his pillows and gazed at her. "Sounds like good riddance to me."

Sarah lifted her shoulders. "I agree—now. At the time, though, it was a little rough." Her brows knitted together, and her eyes grew soft with sympathy. "But not nearly as difficult as losing a spouse must be."

Jake tensed, and a muscle twitched in his jaw. Forcing a light tone, he deliberately steered the conversation away from his marriage. "Well, I hope being here with Nikki and me isn't interfering too much with your love life now."

Her cheeks flushed, fueling his curiosity. He pressed on. "I mean, you probably have a boyfriend or fiancé or someone who might not like you staying out here in the boonies."

"I...I'm not seeing anyone special."

He had no idea why that fact should please him so much.

"Which reminds me," Sarah piped up suddenly. "Your real-estate agent dropped by with a basket of fruit. Said it was a housewarming gift."

Jake grimaced. Sue Ellen Haskell's brazen attempts to catch his eye had made the process of buying the ranch an ordeal. He'd stopped just short of being flat-out rude to the woman, but she refused to take a hint.

"She seemed awfully upset to hear you were injured," Sarah continued. "She said she'd drop by later."

Jake's frown deepened. "I hope you told her not to bother."

"Actually, I told her to stop by tomorrow morning."

"Great," Jake muttered.

The lack of enthusiasm in his voice sent a ripple of pleasure coursing up Sarah's spine. The idea of the buxom blonde cozying up to Jake had bothered her all afternoon, and she was unaccountably relieved to learn that he didn't return the woman's interest.

But only because of Nikki, she told herself sternly. Sue Ellen Haskell didn't strike her as having a maternal bone in her body. "I had no way of knowing you didn't want to see her. The way she made it sound..."

"I can guess how she made it sound," Jake said dryly. "But the fact of the matter is, I have no further business to discuss with Sue Ellen."

Sarah couldn't resist a devilish grin. "I didn't get the impression she was here to discuss business."

Jake's eyebrows drew together darkly. "Well, she's barking up the wrong tree. I'm not looking for a fling. I'm not interested in a relationship, and I darn sure don't intend to ever get married again."

Just as she'd suspected. He'd loved his wife too much to even look at another woman.

Which was just fine, she told herself, deliberately averting her gaze from the dark hair peeking out above the top of his white cotton T-shirt. It didn't matter to her one way or the other. And as for Nikki, the child seemed better off with one parent than many of her students were with two. From the things Nikki had told her about her dad—the way he played with her, joked with her, read to her, and just spent time with her—he sounded exactly like the kind of father she'd always hoped to have for her own children someday.

Not that there was much chance she would ever have children, she thought miserably, swallowing around a hard lump in her throat. That would first require getting married, and her prospects in that department grew increasingly remote with each passing year.

The sobering reality made her heart ball up and drop to somewhere in the vicinity of her stomach. She pulled her gaze away from Jake's right biceps, which bulged in a fascinating manner every time he lifted his fork.

"I'd better go get Nikki's bath ready," she said, ducking out of his room.

Yes, it was certainly a good thing she had none of Sue Ellen's aspirations concerning Jake, she thought as she headed down the hall. A darn good thing, indeed.

Jake limped down the hall two hours later, heading toward the sound of soft voices drifting through the doorway of Nikki's bedroom. Of all the things he'd missed while he was in the hospital, he'd missed Nikki's bedtime ritual of prayers and stories and kisses the most.

"Tell me the princess story again!" he heard Nikki beg.

Jake hesitated outside the door. He recognized the familiar squeak of bedsprings and grinned, knowing Nikki had just hurled herself onto the bed in a running jump as she did every night.

"Okay," Sarah said. "But then you've got to promise to go to sleep."

"All right. I promise."

Jake peered around the door. Sarah was seated in the rocker in the corner. Nikki was stretched out on her tummy, wearing her favorite pink polka-dot pajamas, her head in her hands, her eyes wide and fixed on Sarah. He froze, not wanting to interrupt.

"Once upon time," Sarah began, "there were two little princesses who lived in two far-off lands—Princess Rose of Roseland and Princess Doodle of Doodletown. Princess Rose didn't look much like a princess at all. She dressed in rags, she had freckles on her face and arms, she was tall and skinny, and her only pair of shoes were heavy old brown work boots. Princess Doodle, on the other hand, had gorgeous, porcelain skin....''

''What's pors-lin?'' Nikki asked.

''It's like an old-fashioned doll's face—very smooth and creamy,'' Sarah told her. ''And she had a tiny little princess-like figure, and she dressed in the most magnificent gowns imaginable, decorated with all kinds of precious jewels—rubies and emeralds and sapphires....''

''An' tinklin' diamonds. Don' forget the diamonds that tinkled!''

''All right.'' He could hear the smile in Sarah's voice. ''And twinkling diamonds that sparkled like stars. On her feet were the most delicate high-heeled gold slippers anyone had ever worn.

''It came time for the handsome prince in the neighboring land to choose a bride. So he sent for the two princesses and asked all of their subjects to come and help him decide which princess to marry.

''The mayor of Doodletown stood first and swept his hand toward Princess Doodle, who was dressed in her finest finery. 'As you can see,' he said, 'our princess has lovely skin, a dainty figure, a gorgeous gown, and exquisite golden slippers. Furthermore, she's covered from head to toe with beautiful princess-like jewels. All the world can see she looks exactly like the ideal bride for a handsome prince.'''

Jake grinned at the deep voice Sarah used for the mayor's speech.

''The people all applauded, and the prince said, 'Yes, she is lovely indeed. She looks every inch the princess.'''

To Jake's amusement, Sarah gave the prince a different, more regal inflection.

''Then the mayor of Roseland stood,'' Sarah continued.

"He swept his hand toward Princess Rose, who stood bashfully twiddling her thumbs and staring at the ground.

"'I admit, our Princess Rose doesn't look very royal.'" Sarah presented this character in a weak, high-pitched voice. "'But I'd like to tell you why. She's thin and freckled because she works all day in the hot sun, helping her people tend the fields. Her shoes are heavy and ugly because she walks long distances to visit villagers who are sick or sad in order to help them to feel better.'

"'But she has no jewels!' Princess Doodle protested. 'Everyone knows a princess isn't really a princess unless she has jewels!'"

The raucous squawk of a voice Sarah adapted for the princess made Jake nearly laugh out loud.

Nikki made no effort to suppress her giggles. "Oh, here comes my mos' fav'rit part!" she exclaimed. "I love to hear about the jools!"

Sarah once more pitched her voice to sound like the Roseland mayor's. "'Princess Rose once had the finest jewels in all the world. But she sold them and gave the money to the poor so that everyone in Roseland could have warm homes and clothes and plenty of food to eat.'

"The prince stepped forward. 'It seems to me that there's only one princess here who is truly beautiful. She's the woman I love, and the one I'll marry.'"

"Princess Rose thinks he means Princess Doodle!" Nikki said knowingly.

Sarah nodded. "Princess Rose turned away, feeling very sad. But the prince caught her by the hand. 'Princess Rose, will you marry me?' he asked.

"'But you can't marry her! She's so ugly!' Princess Doodle and the mayor of Doodletown cried.

"The prince put his arm around Princess Rose. 'When I look at her, I see her kind and loving heart, and that makes her the most beautiful princess of all.'"

"The wedding! Don' ferget the part about the wedding!" Nikki urged.

Sarah grinned. "The prince was very wealthy, so he bought farm equipment to help the people of Roseland tend the fields. He built hospitals to care for the sick, and he made sure that no one was poor or hungry. Then he brought in the finest dressmakers and had them create the most magnificent wedding gown ever made. He bought a pair of exquisite crystal slippers and personally put them on Princess Rose's feet. Then he covered her with jewels from head to toe and married her in a big cathedral as all the people cheered. And when he kissed her, he knew in his heart that he was kissing the most beautiful woman in the entire world. And they lived happily ever after."

Nikki sighed and rolled over, her enormous bunny slippers pointing at the ceiling. "Oh, I just love that story! I want to hear it every night for the rest of my life."

Jake stepped into the doorway and grinned. "In that case, you'll need to talk Miss Sarah into writing it down. And I'll probably need a little coaching to get all those voices right."

"Daddy!" exclaimed Nikki, flinging herself off the bed and into his arms.

Above Nikki's curls, Jake saw Sarah rise and turn, her face coloring. "I didn't know you were standing there."

"I didn't want to interrupt." He hugged Nikki. "Besides, Nikki's talked so much about this story that I wanted to hear it for myself."

Sarah's flush deepened. "Nikki, don't wear your father out," she said gently. "And remember, you promised to go right to bed."

"Okay." Nikki sighed as Jake lowered her onto the mattress and helped her remove the slippers.

"Have you already said your prayers?" Jake asked.

Nikki nodded.

"Then you're ready for good-night kisses. How many do you want? Fifteen?"

Nikki's eyes danced with delight at the nightly game. She shook her head, fine white curls flying. "Guess again."

Jake pretended to look puzzled. "Three?"

"Nope."

"Seven? Six? Five?"

"Nope. Keep guessing!"

Jake turned both palms up. "Gee, I don't know. Four?"

Her head bobbed wildly. "One kiss for each candle on my cake."

Jake softly planted two kisses on each pink cheek.

"Don' ferget the extras!"

"I wouldn't dream of forgetting." He gently kissed her forehead twice, then pulled the covers up to her neck and ruffled her baby-fine hair. She was so beautiful, so heart-breakingly sweet, he thought, a lump forming in his throat. The enormity of his love for her swept over him with sudden fierceness. He would do anything—anything at all—to keep her safe, to keep her from ever being hurt. He planted an extra kiss on the top of her curls. "There—all tucked in. Good night, sweetheart."

"Wait!"

Jake turned around in surprise.

"I need four kisses from Miz Sarah, too."

Sarah bent and warmly kissed the child. Nikki's round little arms reached up and hugged her close. Sarah returned the embrace, whispering something in the child's ear that made Nikki giggle.

Mixed feelings roiled through Jake's belly as he watched. Tucking Nikki in at night had always made him feel somehow special and humble and privileged all at the same time. It was odd, sharing the nighttime ritual with someone else. He and Nikki had been doing it alone for all of her life—even when Clarissa was alive.

The thought of Clarissa jabbed like a knife. Steeling his mind against further thoughts of his wife, he stepped into the hall.

Sarah joined him, pulling the door shut behind her. "I thought you were asleep, or I would have asked if you wanted to come tuck her in." Sarah smiled, the expression in her eyes as soft as the fleece on Nikki's bunny slippers. "Bedtime is such a special time with children, don't you think?"

He nodded, liking the way she'd just expressed how he felt. Liking the way she looked in the dim hallway light, her eyes all warm and dreamy behind her glasses. Liking the soft scent of her perfume mingled with the baby powder Nikki drenched herself in after her bath.

His blood pumped harder in his veins, and a dangerous thought formed in his mind. *Bedtime can be pretty special for adults, too.*

Jeezum Pete, he thought with annoyance, raking a hand through his hair. He needed to put a muzzle on his mind.

He cleared his throat and motioned to the stairs. "Sleeping all afternoon seems to have made me hungry. I thought I'd go downstairs and see if there was any more of that chicken."

"There's plenty. But are you sure you feel like dealing with the stairs? I can bring it up to you."

"Actually, I need a little change of scenery. The bedroom walls are starting to close in."

He slowly clumped down the stairs and into the kitchen, then looked around in surprise. The last time he'd seen this room, it had been filled with half-empty boxes.

"Did you unpack the whole house?" he asked.

She paused, her hand on the refrigerator handle. "Pretty much. I hope you don't mind."

"Mind? I think I need to double your salary."

Sarah smiled as she pulled out the covered platter of chicken. Bracing himself against the counter, Jake started opening cabinets, looking for plates. She stepped up to help him and her arm brushed his.

It was an innocent, innocuous touch, purely accidental in nature. It didn't mean anything, and there was no reason at all that it should make his pulse pound, no reason it should warm and electrify the air. No reason that it should make them both freeze, their arms still extended upward, and stare at each other.

He grabbed a plate and cleared his throat. "That story of yours was a real hit with Nikki," he said, leaning against the counter to keep his weight off his injured leg and trying to act as normally as possible. "Where did it come from?"

"I made it up."

"Really?" He watched her turn and extract a fork from a drawer. His eyes followed the way her hair swung when she moved her head, as mesmerized by the movement as he would be by a hypnotist's pendulum. "What inspired it?"

"I had an assignment in the ninth grade to write a paper about my favorite fairy-tale princess. I didn't like any of the princesses in any of the fairy tales I knew, so I made one up."

"You didn't like Cinderella or Snow White or Rapunzel?"

Sarah shrugged. "They were all beautiful. I couldn't relate."

"Why not?"

Sarah stared at him. Was he joking? He'd asked the question so naturally, so sincerely, as if he really didn't have a clue. The expression on his face was equally guileless.

Sarah was so taken aback that she found herself blurting out an explanation. "Well, I'd reached my full height by the time I was thirteen and I towered over all the other kids. On top of that, I was skinny as a rail, with absolutely no signs of physical development. And I had blotchy freckles, funny-looking eyeglasses and braces on my teeth."

Jake grinned as if he found the image amusing. "I went through an awkward stage, too. I remember feeling like the Jolly Green Giant."

Sarah shook her head. "'Awkward' doesn't begin to describe it. But how I looked wasn't the worst of it. My mother was convinced that if she just poured enough effort into it, I would become the graceful, lovely daughter she'd always wanted. She spent hours curling and fixing my hair, patting lemon juice on my skin to bleach the freckles, making me walk with books on my head to correct my posture. She forced me to wear hats when I went outdoors to keep from getting new freckles. She had me drink milk shakes three times a day to try to make me fill out. She sent me to charm school, dance class—" Sarah sighed. "You name it, she tried it."

Jake's eyebrows drew together. "Wow. That must have made you feel awful."

Sarah gave a wan smile. "I know she was only trying to help, but Mom would have done me a much greater service if she'd just taught me to accept myself as I was. Instead, she fussed over me so much, I felt like a freak. That whole experience is one reason I wanted to become a teacher—to help children discover their unique abilities and develop a sense of self-worth that's not based on externals or someone else's opinion."

She looked away, suddenly embarrassed. Good heavens, what had gotten into her, prattling on about herself like that? It was totally out of character. Her thoughts were usually focused on someone or something other than herself.

"Sounds like an important thing for kids to learn. Nikki's lucky to have you for a teacher."

Sarah ventured a glance at him. His eyes were fixed on her face, and the intensity of his gaze made her flush.

"You mentioned that your parents live in Florida," he continued. "Do you see them often?"

Sarah shook her head. "I visit them once a year, and that's about it. They've got a busy social life and travel schedule." She gave a rueful smile. "It's probably just as well. Mom still can't resist trying to make me over."

"I'd think she would be pleased with how you turned out."

"You mean because I'm a teacher?"

"Actually, I was referring to how nice you look now."

Nice. It was a safe, noncommittal word, a word that

could simply mean clean and presentable. But something about the way he'd said it—in the low, silky tone of his voice, in the appreciative gleam in his eye—made her heart race. *Mercy, he made it sound...* Sarah's mouth went dry as her palms grew damp. *He made it sound as if he actually found her attractive!*

The air in the kitchen suddenly seemed to lack sufficient oxygen. She swallowed hard, feeling the old, tongue-tied awkwardness return—the awkwardness that always struck her when she most wanted to be poised and witty. She averted her eyes and rubbed a knot of tension in her neck. "Well, I managed to lose the braces and most of the freckles, but I still don't have much in common with Cinderella."

"Oh, I disagree."

He reached out and lifted a lock of her hair. His touch paralyzed her; she couldn't move, couldn't breathe, couldn't think, couldn't bring herself to look up and meet his gaze even though she could feel the heat of it on her face.

His fingers shifted to the back of her neck and began to gently massage the spot she'd just been rubbing. Her heart stopped, then thrummed against her ribs like the wings of a hummingbird. The fork in her hand shook like a divining rod.

She couldn't tell what was actually happening and what was her imagination. Her emotions were skittering all over the place, making her feel as ungainly and out of control as a first time ice skater. Was he just giving her a friendly neck rub? Or was something deeper, more profound, more sensual going on here?

She needed to know. Swallowing hard, she gathered her courage and forced herself to look into his eyes.

What she saw there made her knees go weak, and she was glad she was leaning against the counter.

Attraction—hot, smoky, intense. It sizzled between them, vibrant and pulsing, with a life of its own.

face was closer than she'd realized, and was getting
r still. The pressure of his fingers on the back of her
neck tightened, and she wasn't sure if she was moving toward him or he was moving toward her. Her blood roared
in her ears, and her mind ceased to function. Her gaze lowered to his lips—lips that looked firm and hungry and so
near, she could almost taste them. Her eyelids fluttered
closed....

"Daddy, can I get a drink of water?"

Sarah jerked her eyes open to see Nikki standing in the
doorway.

Jake whipped around and immediately stepped back. He
drew a deep, shaky breath, his heart hammering in his
chest. "Of course, sweetheart."

He limped toward the cabinets, then realized he had no
idea where Sarah had put the glasses. The woman was con-
founding him at every turn.

"My cups are up there," Nikki said, pointing.

He pulled out a plastic cup with a cartoon character on
it and hobbled to the sink to fill it. When he handed it to
his daughter, he noticed his hand was shaking.

Nikki took a noisy slurp. "What were you and Miz Sarah
doin'?" she asked curiously.

Good question, Jake thought, jamming his fingers
through his hair. Just what the hell *had* he been doing?
Heaven help him, he'd been about to kiss her. Right here,
under the same roof as Nikki.

He stared at his daughter, so small and adorable, clutching her favorite bedraggled bear, and silently swore.

What the hell had he been thinking? Every relationship
eventually broke down or ended. The only way to shield
Nikki from the inevitable pain of being caught in the middle when it did was to never get one started in the first
place.

He'd vowed he would never put Nikki through the mis-
ery he'd gone through as a child—watching two people he
loved quarrel and fight, wanting to comfort them both,

needing comfort himself and having nowhere to turn to get it. And worst of all, feeling somehow responsible for it all.

His experience with his stepmother had been equally painful. And his marriage to Clarissa...

Jake's hands knotted at his sides. He must have lost some of his marbles in that fall, he thought with disgust. Sarah was Nikki's preschool teacher, for heaven's sake, and the child was already attached to her. Of all the people on earth, Sarah was the absolute worst choice for a romantic encounter.

"Sarah and I weren't doing anything. Come on, Nikki. I'll tuck you back into bed," he said abruptly.

He glanced over his shoulder at Sarah as he ushered the child from the room. She stood frozen by the counter, her lips slightly parted, her eyes large and dark and confused. He felt a sharp pang in his chest and silently cursed himself for feeling it.

"Don't bother about the chicken. I've changed my mind." His voice was colder than he'd intended, but it was probably for the best. He needed to keep things between them from getting too personal.

Right, Masters, he told himself sardonically. *The woman rescues your hide, takes care of your daughter, and is nursing your sorry self back to health. Good luck keeping things impersonal—especially when she'll be sleeping just down the hall from you.*

The last thought struck him as disturbingly erotic. He clumped heavily up the stairs, as unsettled as a hungry bull penned next to a field of alfalfa, wondering how on earth he was going to survive the next two weeks.

Chapter Four

"Can I have another Mickey pancake?" Nikki held out her favorite plastic plate, which had a clown face on the bottom. The clown's features were barely visible through a sea of maple syrup.

Nikki's own face was in nearly the same condition, Sarah noted with a grin. "You certainly may. But what's the magic word?"

"Pleeeeaze!"

"Attagirl." Sarah took the plate with one hand and ruffled the child's hair with the other, then headed to the stove to pour batter into the cartoon character-shaped mold on the griddle. She'd bought it at the grocery store earlier in the week when she'd shopped for provisions for Jake's household.

Funny—this warm, fuzzy feeling she got from performing a simple task like fixing the child's breakfast. She loved it. As a matter of fact, she loved this whole situation—taking care of Nikki, tending the house, even doing the laundry. It was easy to pretend it was her home and her child.

Her man.

The thought sent a shiver shimmying up her arms. Nothing, absolutely nothing had ever made her feel the way she'd felt when Jake had rubbed her neck last night.

She'd been kissed before, of course, and when she'd been engaged, she'd even gone a little bit further. But nothing had ever sent prickles of pleasure racing through her like the warmth of Jake's fingers on her skin, the pressure of his touch against her tight tendons. It didn't matter that the only place he'd touched was her neck. He'd made her feel hot and achy and filled with longing in places nowhere near the point of contact.

She could only imagine how she would have felt if he'd pulled her close and claimed her lips with his own. For one incredible heart-stopping moment last night, she'd been certain he'd been about to do just that.

Had he really nearly kissed her? She'd lain awake for most of the night thinking about it, wondering what would have happened if Nikki hadn't interrupted. She'd turned the situation around in her mind, examined it from every angle and played it out to a variety of thrilling conclusions in exquisitely vivid detail.

Sarah gave her head a slight shake and reached for her cup of coffee. She was getting carried away, she chided herself. Nothing had actually happened between them. She was like a child at her preschool, dressing up and playing house in the home center, getting all caught up in a fantasy.

Fantasy. That was what it was, all right—a wonderful, thrilling fantasy.

And that was *all* it was, she told herself sternly. This wasn't her home, Nikki wasn't her child, and Jake sure as heck wasn't her man. He'd paid her one small, polite compliment, and she'd spent the night embroidering it into dozens of exciting, erotic scenarios.

She needed to keep the facts squarely in focus. Jake had no more interest in her than she had in Bad-breath Will. If Jake had felt any attraction to her last night, it was nothing more than hormones and proximity. Under normal circumstances, a man like Jake would never look at her twice. It was a sure bet he would never pick a Plain Jane like her out of a crowd. A man as handsome as Jake could have any woman he chose—a gorgeous woman, a witty woman, a woman lovely enough to win beauty crowns.

A woman like his wife.

The realization sent Sarah's spirits crashing through the hardwood floor. Nikki had proudly shown her a picture of her mother that she kept in her room. Jake's wife had been petite, curvaceous, and beautiful—everything Sarah had ever wished to be and wasn't.

Face it, Sarah. Men like Jake don't fall for women like you. It was a cold, bitter truth; one she'd acknowledged long ago, and one she'd better not let herself forget about now.

Sarah swallowed hard and carefully removed the metal mold from around the pancake. Instead of dwelling on the exquisite sensations Jake's touch had aroused in her, she ought to be thinking about how abruptly he'd pulled away, how quickly he'd headed upstairs, how curtly he'd said good-night. He sure hadn't acted like a man who regretted being interrupted, she thought glumly, sliding a spatula under the half-cooked pancake. On the contrary, he'd acted like a man saved by the bell.

"Good morning."

Sarah jumped at the sound of the deep voice behind her, causing the spatula to jerk upward. She whipped around to find Jake behind her. To her horror, a mouse-eared pancake was plastered to his forehead, dripping batter down his face.

"Daddy, you're wearing Mickey!" Nikki yelped.

"What the..." Jake sputtered, pulling the pancake off his forehead and blinking as batter dripped over his eyes.

Sarah grabbed a damp dish towel and reflexively wiped his face as if he were one of her students. "Oh, I'm so sorry!"

He studied the pancake in his hand, then looked up.

"Are you okay? Are you burned?" Worried, Sarah scrubbed a blob of batter off his eyebrow.

The eyebrow quirked upward. "For a battered man, I'm doing just fine."

The amused twinkle in his eye filled Sarah with relief. She started to smile back, but his eyes locked with hers, and the air in her lungs suddenly evaporated.

There it was again—that strong gravitational pull between them. Her stomach tightened, and her knees turned to putty. Abruptly she realized how close to him she was standing—so close that her breasts pressed against his hard chest and his breath warmed her face. And oh, mercy, her hand still rested on his cheek, her thumb dangerously near his mouth. With just the slightest movement, she could rub it across his lips and feel the texture that had tantalized her thoughts all night long.

He reached out and took the towel from her. Her heart hammering, she pulled away, the rough stubble of his beard prickling her palm as she withdrew it from his face.

She turned back to the stove, cursing herself for a fool and worse, her cheeks burning hotter than the griddle. She didn't know what had rattled her the most: the hard heat of his chest, the look in his eye, the awkward accident, or the memory of her steamy fantasies about him.

"I bet Nikki would prefer to eat her pancakes off that clown's face instead of mine," he remarked.

Nikki dissolved in a fit of giggles.

Sarah mustered a tremulous smile, but her hands shook as she reached for the mold and the bowl of batter. She was all tongue-tied and awkward again—not at all as she'd been in her fantasy encounters with him last night. In her imagination, she'd been sexy and desirable, quick-witted and glib, completely in control of herself and the situation.

In reality, she thought woefully, she couldn't even control a stupid flapjack.

"If you'll have a seat, I'll bring you some orange juice," she said finally.

"I can get it myself."

"But the doctor said you should take it easy."

"I'm temporarily handicapped, not completely incapacitated. A few more steps won't hurt. Besides, it looks like you've got your hands full with Mickey and company."

He brushed against her as he limped to the refrigerator. The contact made her thoughts scatter like startled field mice.

As if on cue, a sharp rapping sounded at the kitchen door. "Yoo-hoo!"

Sarah turned to see Sue Ellen Haskell peering through the glass.

"Yuck! What's *she* doing here?" Nikki scrunched up her face as if she'd just been presented with a bowl of creamed spinach.

Sarah silently echoed the sentiment. The only thing that could possibly make her feel more gauche right now was having the glamorous real-estate agent around to compare herself with. She would bet Sue Ellen was never at a loss for words around a man. With her fluffy blond hair, pretty face and luscious figure, she'd probably never been at a loss for male attention, either.

"She's bringing a housewarming gift," Sarah said.

"Why didn' she just leave it yesterday?" Nikki asked.

"She wanted to deliver it to your father personally." *And have the chance to strut her stuff in front of him again,* Sarah silently added as she opened the door.

Treating Sarah like an invisible servant, the voluptuous blonde pranced her high-heeled way into the room bearing an enormous, cellophane-wrapped fruit basket. Her carefully lipsticked mouth smiled widely at Jake. "Well, I see that our patient is up and about this morning." Her voice was as bright as her lip color and as syrupy as Nikki's plate. "Now, you just stay seated, Jake. No point in straining yourself just to observe protocol."

Sarah looked at Jake as she made her way back to the

stove. As far as she could tell, he'd made no attempt to rise.

Sue Ellen placed the basket in the center of the kitchen table and seated herself beside Jake, making sure that her tight red dress rode high enough to expose a good length of thigh. "How are you feeling this morning?"

"Better." Like his response, his tone was terse.

"I dropped by yesterday, and you could have knocked me over with a feather when your housekeeper told me you'd been in the hospital."

"Sarah's not my housekeeper."

Sue Ellen glanced appraisingly at Sarah, her eyes narrowing like a cat's. Sarah could tell the exact moment Sue Ellen dismissed her as competition. Rankled, Sarah slid the spatula under a pancake and contemplated repeating her earlier mishap. A pair of mouse ears on Sue Ellen's forehead might be just the trick to turn Little Miss Come-Hither into Little Miss Went-Yonder.

"Oh...I'm so sorry. I knew you were looking for some help, Jake, so I just assumed..." Sue Ellen turned and gave Sarah a wide-eyed smile. Sarah was certain the smile was calculated to impress Jake more than to assuage her feelings. "Are you a relative?"

"No. I'm Nikki's preschool teacher. I'm just helping out temporarily."

Sue Ellen glanced at Nikki for the first time since she'd entered the room. "How very nice." Her gaze darted back to Sarah without ever acknowledging the child's presence. "You know, you look familiar." Sue Ellen's brow puckered delicately. "But you're not from around here, are you?"

Something in her tone made Sarah bristle. She'd made it sound as if Sarah didn't belong. "I've only lived here two years, but I used to visit my grandmother in Oak Grove every summer," she said defensively.

Sue Ellen's eyes took on a look of morbid fascination, like those of a person staring at a car wreck. "Oh, now I remember! You're the poor girl who was Tommy Bullock's date at the Fourth of July dance years ago. Oh, that was so awful, the way he—"

Sarah's heart lodged in her throat. *Oh, no, not that topic. Anything but that.*

"That...that was a long time ago," Sarah blurted.

"Yes, it was, but I'll never forget the terrible way he—"

Sarah's blood roared in her ears, and a sense of panic rose in her throat. *I've got to get her off this subject,* she thought frantically, searching her mind for something— anything—to say. "So you're in real estate now?" she interrupted. "You must be very successful to handle big transactions like selling Jake this ranch."

Sue Ellen paused. Her ample chest expanded proudly and her mouth curved into a smug smile. "Well, actually, it so happens I was just named the leading producer for my real-estate firm this month."

Sarah heaved a sigh of relief. Thank heavens the woman was self-centered enough to be easily diverted into talking about what was obviously her favorite topic—herself.

"And I have Jake to thank for that," Sue Ellen continued, turning back to Jake. "In fact, that's why I stopped by. As a way of showing my appreciation, I want to offer you extra services."

Jake lifted a wary eyebrow.

Sue Ellen touched his arm, leaned forward to give him an eyeful of cleavage and laughed as if he'd just said something terribly flirtatious. "To help with the interior of your house, I mean. As I pointed out when I showed you the house, the wallpaper in here and in the master bedroom needs replacing, and several rooms need repainting."

Jake looked around, noting the peeling blue-print wall-paper. He hadn't really given it any thought. He supposed those things were needed, all right, and he admitted he knew less than nothing about them, but he wasn't about to get roped into any further dealings with this hussy. Dealing with Sue Ellen was like being stalked by a hungry she-wolf.

"Thanks, but that's not necessary. I'll handle it myself."

Sue Ellen flashed a beguiling smile. "Between caring for the ranch and your injured leg and your daughter, when are you going to find time? I'll be more than happy to pick up a few paint chips and wallpaper sample books and bring them by this evening."

Jake thought fast. "I'd, uh, planned to ask Sarah to handle all that. She's helped me get settled in and seems to know my tastes."

Sue Ellen shot Sarah a surprised look, her eyes registering clear displeasure. "I see. Well, I didn't realize the two of you had such a special relationship."

"Everythin' Miz Sarah does is special," Nikki chimed in. "'Specially her pancakes and bedtime stories. Right, Daddy?"

If Sue Ellen thought she was going to goad him into saying there was nothing between him and Sarah so she would have another opening to offer her services, she was dead wrong. "Especially the bedtime stories," he agreed with a wicked smile. He glanced up to check Sarah's reaction, but she was fussing at the stove, her back to him.

Sue Ellen gave a plastic smile. "How very…nice." She rose and smoothed her tight, short skirt, then minced to the door. "Well, I really must run. I hope you enjoy your new home." She paused, her hand on the doorknob, and cast him a meaningful look. "If there's ever anything I can do for you, Jake, you've got my number."

"I've got your number, all right," Jake muttered under his breath as the door closed behind her. He looked at Sarah and belatedly remembered her reaction at the hospital when Nikki had proclaimed her to be a live-in friend. He hoped he hadn't embarrassed her again by implying there was more to their relationship than met the eye. "Look, I didn't mean what I just said about asking you to mess with all that stuff."

"I don't mind."

"Interior decorating's not in your job description. I just said that to make her think—"

Think what? That there's something going on between us?

He'd spent half the night trying to keep his thoughts from veering off in that direction, and having Sarah pressed against him this morning, her firm breasts burning holes in his chest, hadn't helped matters in the least. The last thing he needed to do was say anything that would make this damnable attraction between them more of an issue than it already was.

He realized he'd been unconsciously rubbing his chest. He abruptly dropped his hand and cleared his throat. "I just wanted to get rid of her, that's all."

Sarah placed a stack of pancakes in front him, and he caught a tantalizing whiff of her soft perfume. "To tell you the truth, I think choosing paint colors and wallpaper sounds like fun."

Jake shifted uncomfortably in his chair. He didn't know that he liked the idea of Sarah getting any more deeply involved in the workings of his household than she already was. But the prospect of her becoming more deeply entrenched in the workings of his suddenly overcharged hormonal system seemed by far the greater hazard. If she was busy selecting wallpaper and paint in addition to taking care of the house and Nikki, she wouldn't have much time to be playing nursemaid to him.

"Well, if you can find the time, I'd appreciate your help."

"Can we get wallpaper for my room, too?" Nikki asked excitedly. "I want princess wallpaper."

"We'll have to see, Nikki," Jake hedged. "I don't even know if they make the stuff."

Just then, another knock sounded at the door.

"This place is busier than the hospital," Jake muttered.

"It's my partner. She's giving Nikki a ride to pre-school." Sarah crossed the room to open the door.

"Hi, Mrs. Claus!" Nikki called.

"It's Mrs. Kloster," Sarah gently corrected.

"Well, I think it should be Mrs. Claus, 'cause she looks like Santa's wife," Nikki proclaimed.

Deb laughed as she stepped inside. "Why, Nikki, that's the nicest compliment I've had in a long time."

He had to agree with his daughter's assessment, Jake thought, struggling to his feet as Sarah introduced him to the kindly-faced older woman.

Deb waved him back into his seat. "Don't stand on that hurt leg on my account, or Sarah will have my head on a platter. She's a very protective nurse."

He glanced at Sarah in surprise. "She's done this before?"

"She took care of her grandmother even after she was completely bedridden. The rest of her family and the doctors wanted to put her in a rest home, but Sarah wouldn't hear of it. And if any of our students are sick, Sarah always drops by or sends little gifts. She's always doing something for someone. She's got the biggest heart in the world." Deb gazed fondly at Sarah, who was helping Nikki wash her hands at the kitchen sink. When she looked back to Jake, he found himself nailed by the older woman's penetrating gaze. "Sometimes I think she's too kind for her own good. I worry she'll be taken advantage of."

Message received, Jake thought silently. *Don't hurt Sarah.*

Well, he didn't need Deb to tell him that Sarah wasn't the type of woman to fool around with. He chose his words carefully, knowing full well that Sarah was listening to every word, needing to restate the terms of their relationship—as much for his sake as for hers. "That's the last thing I want to do. I appreciate all the help she gave me while I was in the hospital, and it's mighty kind of her to help out until I can get back on my feet. But as soon as I can hire someone to permanently keep house and baby-sit, you'll have your partner back full-time.''

He looked at Sarah, who was stuffing Nikki's favorite teddy bear into the child's book bag. A twinge of warmth spread through his belly. She'd noticed how Nikki liked to clutch the beat-up old animal at nap time and was packing it for her to take to school. It was a little thing, but he was suddenly struck by the thought that it was little things that made a life. Little things like mouse-shaped pancakes and princess bedtime stories and soft, sweet-smelling perfume....

With an effort, he pulled his eyes away and looked back at Deb. "You don't happen to know anyone who might want the job, do you?"

Deb shook her head. "No, but I'll keep my eyes and ears open for you." She turned to Nikki and smiled. "Ready?"

The little girl nodded. "Bye, Daddy." She ran over and hugged him tightly, then scrambled across the room and threw her arms around Sarah. "Bye, Miz Sarah."

"Why don't you walk us out to the car?" Deb said to Sarah.

"Okay." Slinging Nikki's bag over her arm, Sarah cast a glance at Jake. "I'll be right back."

As Nikki scampered ahead to the car, Deb grinned broadly at Sarah, her brown eyes twinkling. "I thought you were carrying your bent for helpfulness a little far when you decided to use your vacation time to help out here, but after meeting Nikki's dad, I don't blame you a bit. He's enough to make even my old ticker do the two-step."

Sarah pulled the book bag's strap up on her shoulder and tried to act unaffected by Deb's observation, but a telltale flush of heat rushed to her cheeks. "Don't be ridiculous."

"There's nothing ridiculous about being attracted to a man, especially a man who looks like that. It's the most natural thing in the world."

"Who said anything about being attracted?"

"Nobody had to say a word."

The temperature of Sarah's face soared. "Is it that obvious?" she moaned softly.

Deb put an arm around her. "Cheer up. I think it's mutual."

Sarah stopped and stared at her friend. "What makes you say that?"

Deb shrugged. "I saw the way he looked at you. It's not the same way he looked at me, I'll tell you that."

A rush of joy gushed into Sarah's veins. Just as suddenly, her self-protective instincts tamped it down.

Deb was mistaken. After all, she was always pushing her to get out and meet men, as if Sarah's only obstacle to matrimony was the fact that she hadn't met a guy terrific enough to fall in love with yet. Deb was such a loyal friend that she had a completely unrealistic view of Sarah's marketability as a single woman.

Sarah shook her head. "I think he's still in love with his late wife. Besides, he's too good-looking, Deb." She gave a sigh of resignation. "There's no way he'd be interested in someone as plain as me."

"How many times do I have to tell you that other people don't see you as you see yourself?" Deb gently scolded. "If you'd just fix yourself up a little—do something softer with your hair, try a little makeup, maybe even wear those contact lenses you've got…"

Sarah stiffened. The suggestions sounded painfully familiar. Her mother had spent years trying to make her over, and the only thing she'd accomplished was to make Sarah feel ugly, inadequate and unlovable.

Well, no more. She'd decided years ago that she wasn't going to pretend to be something she wasn't. Trying to improve her appearance was like trying to force a square peg into a round hole. It didn't work. There was no point in going to a lot of effort just to end up feeling like a failure.

Besides, the only thing worse than being a Plain Jane was being a Plain Jane attempting to look like she wasn't.

Because then she wouldn't be just homely; she would be homely and pathetic.

And maybe even laughable.

The thought sent a shiver up her arm. Sarah stared blankly out at the pastureland beyond the trees and lawn, recalling the exact moment she'd decided to stop trying to improve her appearance, the exact moment she'd given up on makeup and hairstyles and fashion. It had been July fifth of the year she had turned fifteen—the morning after that horrible experience at the dance. The one that Sue Ellen had started to mention this morning...

A cold sweat broke out on Sarah's brow. She wiped it with the back of her hand, wanting to wipe away the painful memory, as well.

From the corner of her eye, she saw Deb studying her curiously. Sarah resumed walking toward the car. "We've been over this before," she said, keeping her eyes fixed straight ahead. "I am what I am. I know what I look like, and I don't need to delude myself into thinking I can look otherwise."

And until now, she thought as she marched down the drive, she'd been okay with that. Until now, she'd been at peace with the fact that most men didn't find her attractive. Until now, she'd been relatively content to fulfill her need to love and be loved by caring for the children at the pre-school and helping others where she could.

But then Jake had entered her life, and all of her hard-won contentment had flown out the window.

A sudden, irrational spark of anger flared within her. How dare he come along and upset her carefully ordered life? She was certain it wasn't entirely her imagination; she was certain that he had, in fact, been flirting with her.

He was probably just toying with her to stay in practice, she thought hotly, like a cat playing with a rubber mouse because he was temporarily housebound. The moment he could get out and play the field, he would abandon her for choicer prey in nothing flat.

Sarah's fingers curled into tight balls. She knew handsome men were usually lowlifes and heels. At the very least, they tended to place too much value on looks—both their own and everyone else's. Why did she think Jake was any different?

Well, it was a darn good thing she'd come to her senses before she'd made a fool of herself. She only hoped her misplaced attraction wasn't as obvious to Jake as it had been to Deb.

"You'd better get going or you'll be late," she told her partner, handing her Nikki's bag.

"All right. Have a nice day with the Incredible Hunk!" With a frisky wink, Deb climbed into the car.

Sarah waved at Nikki, who had already strapped herself into the back seat of the car, then turned and went to face the man who'd had her head in the clouds ever since she'd first laid eyes on him.

Only now, thanks to Sue Ellen and the painful memory she'd raised, Sarah had had a reality check. From here on out, she intended to keep her feet firmly planted on the ground.

Chapter Five

Jake stared at the cattle-auction flyer on his desk and shifted in his burgundy leather chair, trying to find a more comfortable position for his injured leg. He'd been sitting here in his home office since lunch, his leg propped on a footstool under his desk. He'd tried sorting through his mail and concentrating on paperwork, but his mind kept drifting to the woman who was softly humming across the hall.

He wasn't actually bothered by the sound of her humming, he realized. On the contrary, he liked it.

And that was the problem. The fact that he liked it made it distracting. For that matter, *everything* about the woman was distracting.

And it wasn't even her fault, he thought with a scowl. Over the course of the past two days, she'd been all but invisible. During the day when they were alone together, she checked in every couple of hours to see if he needed anything, but otherwise, she made herself scarce. She disappeared the moment he entered a room, scurried around corners to keep from encountering him in the hall, and avoided eye contact when she brought him lunch. With Nikki, however, she was as warm and affectionate as ever.

He'd spent an inordinate amount of time wondering if he'd done something to offend her, and another ridiculously large chunk of time wondering why he cared. He'd decided he was going to keep his distance from her, anyway. It should make no difference that she'd beat him to the punch.

But it did. And it bothered the dickens out of him that he'd developed the annoying habit of looking at his watch, anticipating when she would next appear to perform her duty. He glanced at his watch now, noting that she was overdue.

A soft rap sounded at the door. It was about time, he thought grumpily.

"Come in."

Sarah stood in the doorway, her back ramrod straight, her hair pulled back from her face with those ever-present barrettes, wearing a shapeless blue shirt and a baggy pair of jeans. He wondered for the umpteenth time why she always wore clothing that hid her figure. From what he could discern, she had nothing to hide.

As if she could read his thoughts, she crossed her arms protectively in front of her. The tart scent of lemon furniture polish drifted from the feather duster in her hand. "Can I do anything for you?"

"As a matter of fact, you can." Jake swung his leg off the footstool and rose heavily from his chair. "I need a ride out to the cattle pens. The men are supposed to have rounded up all the weaned calves. I need to look them over and decide which ones to keep and which to sell at auction."

Her expressive face registered first surprise, then concern. "Are you sure you're up to that?"

"Sure." He leaned heavily on the back of the chair to keep his weight off his injured leg.

Sarah saw his knuckles whiten as he gripped the chair.

She eyed him dubiously. "I don't know. The doctor said for you to take it easy."

"And I have been."

"How's your head?"

"Fine."

"It doesn't hurt anymore?" Something about the stiff way he was holding it made her sure that it did. "What about your leg? And your shoulder?"

"They're going to feel the same whether I'm indoors or out." Jake's voice was gruff, his mouth set in a determined line. "Are you going to give me a ride, or do I have to drive myself?"

"You can't drive with your leg like that!"

"If you don't stop arguing about it and agree to give me a lift, we'll get to find out."

Jake clumped toward the door. Bristling at his brusque behavior, Sarah stepped back to let him through and caught a whiff of his after-shave cream as he brushed past. The faint, woodsy scent triggered something deep in her stomach, making her feel everything that she'd tried so hard *not* to feel for the past three days.

The unwanted pull of attraction increased her sense of irritation. Setting the duster on a side table, she followed him down the hall.

"We'll take the truck," he said curtly. "Parts of that back road are pretty rough." He grabbed the keys from a hook by the kitchen door and limped outside, pausing to hold the door open for her before heading for the pickup.

He grimaced as he struggled to climb into the passenger seat. His injured leg and shoulder made the high step up difficult, Sarah realized. She watched him grab the top of the cab with his left hand and awkwardly try again. She could tell from the expression in his eyes that the effort was costing him.

It probably served him right, but she couldn't bear to see him in pain. "Let's take my car," she suggested. "It'll be easier for you to get in and out."

"I can make it." His lips pale from the effort, he managed to swing into the seat. He reached down and dragged his hurt leg into the cab like a deadweight behind him.

He was stubborn—more so than she would have imagined. Sarah didn't know why the fact filled her with grudging admiration; probably because she was that way herself.

He looked down, his hand on the open door, and angled a roguish grin at her. "I seem to have forgotten my manners. I hope you'll excuse me for not getting out to open your door."

His smile burned away her irritation like sunshine on early-morning fog. Relieved that he hadn't aggravated his injuries, Sarah grinned back. "My grandmother used to say you could always tell a patient was getting better when he started getting ornery."

"Ornery—is that what I'm being?"

"Among other things."

Jake rubbed his jaw and gave her a rueful smile. "Guess I've been called worse." Sarah rounded the truck and climbed into the driver's seat, inordinately pleased at having made him smile.

"Hey, I'm sorry if I was rude," he said when she settled behind the wheel. "Fact is, I've got to check these calves today whether I feel like it or not. The ranch doesn't stand still just because I got hurt."

He handed her the keys. They were warm with the heat of his hand, and the warmth spread up her arm and through her chest. Unnerved by the reaction, she awkwardly inserted the key in the ignition and started the truck. The pickup jerked forward. Feeling as unsteady as the vehicle, she searched her mind for something to say as she guided the truck down the gravel drive.

"How did you end up in ranching?"

Jake shrugged. "Guess it's in my blood. My dad was a rancher, and his dad was one before him. I never really considered doing anything else."

Sarah glanced over at him in surprise. He was better

looking than most of the men pictured on billboard adver-
tisements. She'd halfway expected Jake to say he'd made
a stab at acting or modeling or some other career based on
looks and charm. "Did your mother come from a ranching
family, too?"

Jake gave a derisive snort. "Hardly. Mom was a real city
gal. Her father was a diplomat, so she was accustomed to
traveling and entertaining and all that other high-society
stuff. She never got the hang of rural life."

"Is that what broke up your parents' marriage?"

"Pretty much. Mom was lonesome and bored, and it
probably didn't help matters that our ranch was forty-five
minutes from town. She wanted Dad to sell the ranch and
move to the city. I remember hearing horrible arguments.
I remember thinking it was all my fault."

Sarah's heart turned over. "That's a typical reaction for
a child to have. It's so hard on children when their parents
argue."

A nerve flexed in his jaw. "Yeah, well, take it from me,
it's even worse when their parents divorce. I was only eight,
but I remember feeling like my world had broken apart
when Mom moved away. My folks were supposed to share
custody, but I didn't feel at home at either place. I kept
thinking that if I'd been a better kid, Mom wouldn't have
left."

Sarah pulled her eyes from the road and glanced at him,
a lump in her throat. Jake was staring out the window, his
face averted.

"How did your dad handle it?"

Jake shrugged. "He was always quiet. After Mom left,
he just got quieter. He didn't have much of an idea how to
deal with a kid. I think he married my stepmother for my
sake, to give me a mom." His mouth pulled into a humor-
less smile. "Boy, was that ever a mistake."

"Why? What was she like?"

Jake rubbed his jaw. "Oh, she wasn't abusive in any
way. She just never had much use for me, that's all. But I

guess it's hard to get attached to a child who's not your own."

"That's not always the case," Sarah said, hating for him to indict all second marriages on the basis of one bad experience. "I've had students with wonderful stepparent relationships."

"Well, I intend to make sure Nikki never has to worry about it."

The statement had the firm, flat ring of finality. Sarah sneaked a glance at his profile, noting the rigid set of his jaw, then gazed back at the dirt road, mulling over his words. He'd just talked pretty freely about his childhood, despite the fact that it had evidently been a painful one. But every time the topic of his wife came up, he locked up tighter than a bank at quitting time.

The real reason Jake was so determined not to remarry probably had a lot more to do with his own marriage than with his parents' divorce and his stepmother's indifference, Sarah mused.

She guided the truck along the bumpy road, wondering what it would feel like to love so completely, wondering if Jake's wife had appreciated the depth of his feelings for her, wondering if she'd loved him as much as he'd evidently loved her. And as she wondered, she was stabbed by an irrational flash of jealousy.

The emotion caught her off guard, and she was still struggling to tamp it down when Jake pointed to a large metal-roofed structure flanked by a labyrinth of post-and-wood fencing. "The pens are up ahead."

Breathing a sign of relief, Sarah pulled up beside a large corral filled with mewling calves. The two ranch hands, Hank and Buddy, leaned against the gate, their horses tethered to the fence. They doffed their hats at Sarah as she killed the engine, their grizzled faces creasing into grins. Sarah waved and smiled back. The two older men were unfailingly polite to her and Nikki when they stopped by the house each evening to meet with Jake, and Sarah made a point of seeing to it that she had a fresh pot of coffee and a plate of homemade cookies to offer them.

"This shouldn't take too long," Jake said, managing the climb down from the truck much more easily than he'd handled the climb in.

Rolling down her window, she watched him hobble over to the two men, who were just out of earshot. After conferring briefly with Jake, Hank climbed on his horse and rode into the pen while Buddy loped behind. Leaning heavily on the fence, Jake pointed to a calf. Hank's horse skillfully cut the animal away from the herd and hustled it into the chute, where Buddy closed the gate. The three men repeated the routine for the next half hour until Jake gave a satisfied nod. Limping heavily, he walked over to the smaller pen and inspected the dozen animals he'd selected.

Sarah watched him run his hands along an animal's spine, then hold its head to examine its eyes and mouth. He looked capable, confident, in charge—like a man who knew exactly what he was doing. From the respectful expression on his two ranch hands' faces, they evidently thought so, too.

Which said quite a bit about him, Sarah reflected, rattled by the thought; Hank and Buddy had probably been working ranches since before Jake was born.

He grimaced as he leaned down to inspect the animal's limbs, the pain of bending his injured leg evident on his face. After checking every calf in the pen in a similar fashion, he finally nodded, shook the two men's hands and hobbled back to the truck.

He looked tired, Sarah observed, worrying how he was going to get back into the truck. She was relieved when he pulled a wooden crate out of the pickup bed, threw it on the ground and used it as a stepping stool.

"Sorry to make you wait," Jake said, settling himself beside her on the gray vinyl seat.

"That…that's okay," Sarah said, suddenly overwhelmed by his nearness, by the scent of sunshine and dust and sweat that clung to him, by the fact that it hadn't bothered him in the least to use the crate to help himself get back into the truck. His actions told her that he wasn't at all worried about looking macho.

But then, he had no reason to worry about looking it; he *was* macho—the very embodiment of the word.

The thought made her heart race. She swallowed nervously, trying to quiet the insane surge of attraction eddying in her belly. "That was fascinating to watch."

He gave a tight smile. "Maybe so, but I'm not big on watching. I missed being the one on horseback."

With a disconcerted smile, Sarah started the truck engine. Seeing him at work had somehow changed everything. She could no longer tell herself he was nothing but a handsome hunk of beefcake. Not when he was so obviously in control of his business, so respected by his staff. Not when he'd ignored what must be excruciating pain in order to do what needed to be done.

She'd been unfairly prejudiced against him because of his looks, she realized with chagrin. She'd assumed that a man as good-looking as Jake would avoid responsibility, would shirk from hard work, would look for the easy way out.

She'd done him a terrible injustice, she thought, feeling small-minded and petty and thoroughly ashamed of herself. She'd done the very thing she'd always resented people doing to her—she'd discounted him because of his appearance.

She was guilty of looks discrimination.

As much as the realization bothered her, another realization bothered her even more. If he wasn't all the negative things she'd told herself he must be, then he was more attractive than ever.

Her heart sinking she clung to the steering wheel as if it were a life preserver. She thought she felt Jake's eyes on her, but she resisted the urge to glance over and check. Her imagination was probably just working overtime again. After all, her overactive imagination was a major reason why she'd been plagued with this unreasonable attraction to him even while telling herself he was no doubt lazy and spoiled. How on earth was she going to deal with it now that she knew he wasn't?

The truck bounced hard as she turned into the gravel drive leading to the house. She heard the dull thud of Jake's shoulder hitting the door and his sharp inhalation of breath. She glanced at him worriedly. "Are you okay?"

He gave a single, curt nod, but the hard set of his mouth told her he was in pain. "Should have buckled my seat belt," he muttered. "I've got a shoulder-strap adjuster on it for Nikki, so I didn't bother with it."

Oh, great. Go ahead and remind me that you're a terrific father, she thought morosely. It was bad enough that she was playing house with the most gorgeous hunk of manhood she'd ever set eyes on, knowing full well that a man who looked like Jake was never going to be interested in a woman as plain as her. She might not like it, but it was a fact she'd long ago accepted.

What was completely, thoroughly unacceptable—not to mention grossly, rottenly unfair—was the fact that he was turning out to be an all-around wonderful guy.

She sneaked another glance at him. The stoic set of his jaw as he silently clutched his injured shoulder spoke louder than a moan of pain. She needed to be worrying about his physical well-being instead of obsessing about his physical assets, she chided herself. The poor man was plenty banged up, and he'd hired her to help out while he healed. Instead of helping, she'd just added to his injuries. "I'll try to drive more carefully," she promised.

She was relieved when they reached the house. Sitting beside him in such close proximity had severely jangled her nerves. Her palms were sweating, and her stomach felt like she'd swallowed a bowl of rocks. Turning off the engine, she scrambled out of the cab. "I'll get the door for you."

"There's no need," he replied, but she'd already slammed the truck door closed.

Jake massaged his shoulder and muttered an oath as she circled to the passenger side. If he hadn't been staring at her like a loon in mating season, he would have known they were coming up on that infernal bump in the road back there and braced himself for it.

He seemed to lose track of his surroundings when she was around, he thought with self-contempt. He'd prattled on like a blithering idiot on the drive out to the pens, then couldn't think of single thing to say to her on the way back. Something about her made him just zone out. It wouldn't surprise him if Rod Serling appeared on his porch and announced he'd just entered the Twilight Zone. On second thought, he would probably call it the Erogenous Zone.

Hell, he was zoning out now, just sitting here, letting her wait on him hand and foot. He shook his head in self-disgust, jerked the door open, and eased out on his good left leg. He faltered as he hit the ground. Sarah rushed up to steady him but only succeeded in throwing him farther off balance. The next thing he knew, he was in her arms—and they were belly to belly, chest to chest, their faces just inches apart.

"Are...are you all right?" she asked breathlessly.

How would he know? He couldn't form a coherent thought to save his life. All he could do was stare and feel—stare at the concerned expression in her incredible eyes, at the way her long eyelashes swept her glasses every time she blinked; feel her hands on his back, her breath on his face, her pelvis against his.

He eased away to keep her from detecting his body's response. "I'm fine."

But he sure didn't feel it. He was having trouble breathing, and it had nothing to do with his injuries. He cleared his throat.

"I...I'll help you inside," she said, putting her arm around him.

He knew he should protest. After all, he was perfectly capable of making it on his own. But the feel of her against him was too exquisite a sensation to surrender. As unwise as he knew it was, he looped his arm around her waist and leaned against her as they made their way through the kitchen door.

"Do you need to go to bed?" she asked.

Do I ever. He swallowed convulsively.

"I think you overdid it this afternoon. A rest would probably do you good."

Jake managed a nod.

"I'll help you to your room."

Jake shamelessly allowed her to do just that. He tilted into her as they headed for the staircase, reveling in the way her hair smelled like an earthy bouquet of herbs and flowers, in the way her arm felt around him, in the way her hip bounced against his with every step.

"Does your head hurt?" Her eyes were amazing, he thought distractedly—as soft and gray as a dove's feather, as warm as a down comforter. And filled with worry.

Worry over him. A ripple of warmth rushed through him at the recognition.

"Not as bad as other parts," he answered carefully.

"I'm sorry about your shoulder. How's your leg?"

He was more concerned with her leg, which was brushing against his thigh in a slow, delicious rhythm as they moved together up the stairs. "I...I probably need to get off it for a while."

He definitely needed to get his mind off her and the sensations she was arousing in him, but he was completely mesmerized by the feel of her body against him. At last, they made their way to the top of the stairs, then down the long hallway to the master bedroom. "Here we are," she said, easing him through the door and to the edge of the bed.

He hesitated. He knew she expected him to sit down, but he was reluctant to break contact with her. The very thought of relinquishing his hold on her waist made his fingers involuntarily tighten around it.

Her eyes widened and locked with his as he gripped her, and he knew the exact moment her surprise blazed into something else. The very air in the room seemed to ignite like a flammable vapor. Her chest rose, her breath caught, and her lips parted.

Those parted lips were his undoing. Without pausing to consider his actions, he hauled her against him, claimed her mouth with his own and pulled her down with him as he sank to the bed.

Her lips were the texture of wet silk. Sweet and salty and hot, they flowered under his—opening and moving and sliding, hesitantly at first, then with increasing need. She moved against him, wrapping her arms around his back. The sheer, erotic pleasure of her body against his blew all coherent thought from his mind.

This was not the smooth, practiced kiss of a woman who knew what she was doing. This was the nose-bumping, glasses-poking kiss of a woman without much experience in this arena—a woman who had no knowledge of her own appeal, no concept of pacing or technique, no idea of what her raw, naked hunger was doing to him.

No idea that she was driving him completely out of his ever-loving mind.

Never in his entire life had a kiss inflamed him so. His blood pounded in his veins like molten lava, thick and hot and fast. He was on fire. He was a human blast-furnace. He was beyond thinking, beyond reason. He was pure, blind, torrid need, and Sarah's need seemed to match his own.

He leaned over her, pressing her back against the mattress, unable to resist her lips or her warm breasts against his chest or the way her hands were roaming his back. She was exquisite. She was exciting beyond belief. He opened his eyes and gazed down at her and was thrilled to find her own eyes open and looking back. She was an intuitive lover, in sync with his every move. She was an unknowing siren, an innocent enchantress, a white-hot, virginal temptation....

Unknowing. Innocent. Virginal. Slowly the words penetrated the steamy fog now filling the space his brain had once occupied.

Suffering cow patties. What the hell was he doing?

He pushed himself off her. "I...I'm sorry," he mumbled. "I didn't mean... I mean, I don't want..."

Passion-dazed and confused, she stared up at him.

"I can't... I mean, we shouldn't..." he muttered.

Comprehension filled her eyes, along with something else. Hurt.

Guilt knotted his gut. Oh, criminy. He'd never meant to hurt her, and from the look on her face, he'd wounded her to the core. He didn't quite understand how, but he darn sure needed to try to rectify the situation. "Hey... I...I'm sorry," he repeated. "Are you okay?"

She rolled away and sat on the edge of the bed, her back toward him. He stared at her thin shoulders, feeling lower than a prairie dog's tunnel, wondering why she seemed so devastated. After all, she'd been kissing him just as fervently as he'd been kissing her.

He hesitantly reached toward her, his hands hovering over her arms. When he finally touched her, she flinched and drew away.

He swallowed hard and tried again. "Look, I don't know what happened. I got carried away. I didn't mean to—"

But he was talking to the door. As she slammed it behind her, a whoosh of air fanned across the room, hitting him like an Arctic blast. He sat on the rumpled bed and gazed at the door, silently calling himself every name in the book.

"Oh, pleeeeaze," Nikki wheedled. "Just one more time." The little girl gazed up at Sarah pleadingly, her head in her hands as she sprawled, tummy down, on her bed.

Sarah sighed. Ordinarily she didn't mind repeating the

princess story, but this evening the tale was sticking in her craw. She patted the little girl's back. "It's getting late, Nikki. Once is enough for tonight."

"Maybe you can just tell the ending. The part where the prince knows she's bootiful."

Fat chance a prince would ever see beyond the princess's appearance, Sarah thought bitterly. *Men weren't made that way. Especially not men like Jake.*

One minute he'd been kissing her like there was no tomorrow, and the next he'd opened his eyes. Getting a good look at her must have spoiled whatever fantasy he'd been having, Sarah thought hotly, because the next thing she knew, he'd backed away as if she'd suddenly sprouted a mustache and horns.

Speak of the devil. As if she'd summoned him, Jake limped into the room.

"Miss Sarah's right, sweetheart. It's getting late. Ready to read a storybook?"

Sarah hated the way her pulse accelerated at the sight of him. With as much dignity as she could muster, she rapidly retreated to the far side of the room. She'd managed to steer clear of him all afternoon and had invented an errand in town in order to avoid having dinner with him, but it was inevitable she would encounter him here tonight. They'd fallen into the routine of tucking Nikki into bed together.

Unless she wanted to upset the child, she would have to act as if nothing had changed. Jake had evidently decided the same thing. She should have known he was too good a father to let anything interfere with his daughter's bedtime ritual.

Well, if he could act like nothing had happened between them, she could, too. Sarah forced herself to remain in the room, to sit calmly in the rocking chair in the corner, to keep her face impassive as Jake sat beside Nikki and read *Goldilocks and the Three Bears.*

But her feelings were far from impassive. Despite her

best intentions, she found herself viewing him differently, noticing things she hadn't seen before.

Things like his work-hardened hands. They were tanned and large and slightly callused on the pads of his palm. They somehow looked different, now that she knew how they felt running along her spine, pulling her against him, pressing her down on the mattress.

And the stubble of his beard. Funny, but she'd never noticed before how it made the cleft in his chin seem more pronounced or how it shadowed his jaw. But then, she'd had no idea before how it felt under her fingers, or how the rasp of it against her face raised goose bumps of pleasure.

And then there was his mouth. She'd studied it before, fantasizing how it would feel to kiss him. But it somehow looked different, now that she knew.

Her stomach knotted in a tight ache. She crossed her arms and pressed them against it.

The awful part was how wonderful that kiss had been, she mused woefully. Beyond wonderful; beyond words. It was fireworks and earthquakes and symphonies and cyclones. Now she understood what all the fuss was about— what all those poets and musicians and writers were trying to describe.

She'd felt connected to him on a whole other plane. For every exquisite physical sensation his kiss had generated, she'd felt a corresponding emotional one. That kiss had been the most amazing experience of her life—a real eye-opener.

Until Jake had opened *his* eyes, that was.

A painful sense of inadequacy stabbed her. Odd, the way two people could share such an intimate act and come away with entirely different takes on the experience.

She'd never wanted the kiss to end.

He'd evidently wished it had never started.

She was drawn to him despite his attractiveness.

He'd been stopped cold by her lack thereof.

A lump formed in Sarah's throat. She really should be

beyond this by now, she told herself sternly. She knew men didn't find her appealing. But somehow Jake had gotten through her usual defenses, making her hope...

Hope what? She knew better than to hope for what she couldn't have. This was what she got for pretending—even for a moment—that things were other than they were.

But knowing she was a fool didn't make Jake's rejection hurt any less.

"Night, sweetheart." The words jerked Sarah back to the present, and she was suddenly aware that Jake was bestowing a last good-night kiss on Nikki's forehead.

Nikki stretched out her arms. "Your turn, Miz Sarah!"

Sarah waited until Jake headed for the door before she crossed the room to hug the child. "Good night, honey." Sarah planted four tender kisses on the little girl's cheeks. Whatever her feelings might be for Nikki's father, the child was an absolute angel.

Sarah dawdled as long as she could, plumping Nikki's pillow and smoothing her blankets, wishing Jake would disappear and she wouldn't have to deal with him any further tonight. But when she finally pulled the door shut behind her and stepped into the hall, Jake was leaning against the wall, waiting.

She tried to brush past him.

"Sarah... Wait."

She would have kept going, but he reached out and caught her by the wrist. "We need to talk."

His grip was light, but it burned like a brand. Sarah averted her eyes, not wanting him to see the effect he was having on her. "There's nothing to say."

"Yes, there is. I feel like the world's biggest heel. I was out of line this afternoon, and I'm really sorry for what happened."

Sarah bit her lip, briefly closing her eyes. This was all too humiliating. She didn't have much in the way of an ego, but she did have some pride. Standing here listening to him tell her how much he regretted what was the most glorious moment of her life was enough to make her want to burst into tears.

Well, she would be darned if she would let him know it. She intended to preserve some small shred of dignity. The best way to cope with this situation was to act completely unaffected.

She drew a deep breath, straightened her posture, stepped back, and extricated her arm. "Don't worry about it. It was just one of those things. It's no big deal."

His brow furrowed. He shoved his hands into his jeans pockets, looking thoroughly disconcerted. "Well, I want to reassure you it won't happen again. I mean, I know things are little awkward between us, but you don't have to keep going out of your way to avoid me. I promise to behave from now on."

Sarah waved her hand dismissively. "It was nothing. I haven't given it another thought."

He stared at her, his eyes dark and narrowed, his mouth tight. With no small measure of satisfaction, Sarah noticed a nerve twitch in his jaw.

Good, she thought. *Maybe you'll lie awake worrying that you've lost your touch.*

Sarah lifted her head to what she hoped was a regal angle and leveled a cool gaze at him. "If you don't need anything further from me tonight, I think I'll turn in early." Without waiting for his response, she swept past him and strode down the hall.

Jake's fingers dug into his palms as he watched her go. *Nothing?* She thought that mind-boggling, sanity-erasing, toe-curling kiss was *nothing?*

He had half a mind to chase after her, kiss her again, and see if she would still say the same thing.

He stopped himself short of doing just that. Bracing his hands against the wall, he shook his head in disgust. Jee-zum Pete, he was losing it. He'd castigated himself all afternoon for kissing her, then forced himself to apologize for it. Yet here he was, ready and eager to make the same mistake all over again.

And it *was* a mistake, he reminded himself. A terrible one. There was only one direction a relationship with a woman like Sarah could take, and he would be damned if he would ever get caught in that trap again. As the old saying went, "Fool me once, shame on you. Fool me twice, shame on me." Just the thought of marriage brought a bitter taste to his mouth.

Why was he even standing here thinking about it? It wasn't like they were having an affair or anything. He was making too big a deal of it. All they'd shared was one little kiss.

A little kiss that had rattled his teeth, rotated his tires, and left him feeling like bale of hay hit by a twister.

Jake ran a hand down his face and exhaled harshly. Hell's bells! He wasn't a good enough liar to convince himself that kissing Sarah hadn't been something special. And he didn't believe for one second that she was unaffected by it, either. On the contrary, he would bet dollars to doughnuts that she'd been just as caught up in it as he'd been. Why, just the memory of the way she'd responded was enough to get him steamed up all over again.

With a disgusted shake of his head, he turned and stormed down the hallway as fast as his wounded leg would allow. He needed to just forget about it, he told himself. He would put it completely out of his mind. He wouldn't allow himself to think about the sweet slide of her lips on his, or how her eyes had grown soft and smoky, or how her soft, supple curves had burned their imprint on his body.

He would pretend it hadn't happened. He would simply block it out, he thought firmly, slamming the door to his bedroom behind him with more force than required—reminding him, to his chagrin, of exactly the way Sarah had slammed it earlier.

Chapter Six

"I'm ready to plant the 'chini!" Nikki called.

Sarah looked over at the child, who was crouched on all fours in the freshly-tilled backyard garden, proudly beaming at a scraggly row of odd-size holes and wearing most of the soil she'd excavated.

"I got the holes all dug. See?" Nikki brushed a strand of hair from her eyes, adding yet another streak of dirt to her face.

Sarah's grin widened. "Good job. I'll go get the seed packets and the watering can."

Thank heaven for weekends, Sarah thought, putting down her hoe and heading for the gardening supplies she'd laid out on the patio. She was delighted to have the child around full-time. Not just because she adored her, but because the girl diverted her from constantly thinking about Jake.

They'd settled into a pattern of avoidance ever since that disturbing kiss, with both of them trying to stay out of each other's way. Sarah was beginning to wonder if the kiss had actually happened or if it had all been a product of her imagination. Jake had acted so curt and aloof for the past four days that it seemed impossible he'd ever demonstrated any interest in her.

He certainly didn't have any interest in anything she was doing around the house, Sarah thought irritably, pulling off her cotton gardening gloves and wiping her brow with the back of her hand. She'd shown him several wallpaper samples for the kitchen and Nikki's bedroom, and he'd barely glanced at them. "They're fine. Whatever you pick will be okay with me," he'd said. She'd gotten similiar responses to questions about meal and laundry preferences. The man obviously didn't want to be bothered with domestic issues—unless they pertained to Nikki.

When it came to his child, he was all tenderness and attention. Sarah had watched the two of them joking and roughhousing in the den just that morning, and she'd gotten so misty-eyed she'd had to leave the room. It was wonderful, seeing how much Jake loved his daughter—how his eyes lit up when she walked into the room, how easily he would drop a kiss on her head or reach out to ruffle her hair, how often he would stop what he was doing to help her with a puzzle or read her a story. He was a terrific father, and Nikki was one lucky kid to have him as a parent. But even as glad as she was for Nikki, she sometimes felt an odd little twinge of wistfulness.

Why couldn't he be tender with her, too?

That line of thinking would get her nowhere, Sarah scolded herself, shoving a couple of packets of seeds into the pocket of her loose-fitting jeans. Jake had no interest in her except as a housekeeper and baby-sitter and preschool teacher. That kiss had been an aberration—a bit of momentary insanity that had happened while he was probably thinking about his late wife.

She picked up the watering can and headed purposefully for the faucet. She was doing the right thing, trying to avoid him, she reassured herself. Not that it was always possible;

the nature of her job occasionally threw them alone together.

Yesterday, for example, she'd had to drive him to the doctor's office to have his stitches removed. On the way into town, they'd made stiff, polite conversation about impersonal topics such as the weather and local politics. On the trip back, they'd loosened up enough to discuss movies and books and music, but a level of tension existed between them that made Sarah as jumpy as a June bug. Whenever she was around him, her heart pounded, her palms sweated, and she found it hard to breathe—much less think.

Well, she wouldn't have to put up with it much longer, Sarah thought, bending to turn on the faucet beside the patio. Jake had completely recovered from the concussion, his shoulder was better and his leg was healing well. The doctor had said he could resume most of his normal activities soon. As it was, he didn't seem to need any personal help from her anymore. For the past three mornings, Buddy had picked him up in his truck before sunrise and Jake had spent the entire day out on the ranch, not returning to the house until dinnertime.

In any event, the ad for a permanent housekeeper would run soon. He would probably hire someone in the next few days. By the end of next week, her stint here would be over.

But for some reason, the knowledge failed to comfort her. She should be glad to be out of this nerve-racking situation, she chided herself. She would still get to see Nikki at preschool, and Nikki was the only reason she'd ever offered to help Jake out in the first place—at least, that was what she wanted to believe. She didn't know why the thought of leaving should have her feeling so depressed.

It must be that silly fairy tale, she told herself, shutting off the faucet. She'd repeated it to Nikki so often that she was probably starting to believe it herself.

"Daddy!"

Sarah straightened as Jake rounded the corner of the

house. He still walked with difficulty, but his limp was growing less pronounced with every passing day.

Nikki sat back on her heels and waved a muddy hand. "Lookee, Daddy! Miz Sarah and I are plantin' a garden wif veg'ables an' flowers. An' I dug the holes!"

Jake cast a glance at Sarah as he stopped beside her. "You didn't say anything to me about a garden."

Oh, dear. She could tell from the way his lips were pressed in a tight line that he wasn't pleased. "It's a wonderful educational activity," she said defensively, balancing the heavy watering can with both hands. "Since the garden plot was already here, I didn't think you'd mind."

"Well, it just so happens I do." Even to his own ears, Jake knew he sounded unreasonable. The realization only heightened his sense of irritation.

The problem wasn't the garden. It was the way Sarah was weaving herself into the very fabric of his life, more and more tightly all the time. And it was his own darn fault. He should have kept a firmer rein on her, but in order to do so, he would have had to interact with her more. And he hadn't trusted himself to do that.

Besides, she had the house running as smoothly as a new tractor, and Nikki had never seemed happier or more secure.

But a garden... That was a long-term project. The idea of Sarah and anything long-term alarmed him. She'd only be here a little over a week more, and he was already wondering how he and Nikki were going to get along when she left. Whoever he hired to replace her was going to seem like nothing but a poor substitute.

"You haven't shown much interest in other household affairs, so I didn't bother to ask you about it," Sarah was saying, her chin tipped up at a stubborn angle. "And as you can see, Nikki's very enthusiastic about the idea."

Jake's own chin tilted up just as stubbornly. "A garden requires a lot of upkeep, and I don't have time to fool with it."

"I'll take care of it, Daddy." Nikki had joined them on the patio. "An' Miss Sarah will help."

Jake stared pointedly at Sarah before turning back to Nikki. "Miss Sarah won't be here much longer, honey."

"Well, she'll come visit, won't she?"

Criminy. How was he supposed to answer that?

Sarah set the watering can down on the picnic table and patted the child's back. "I'll see you at school every day. And I'll bet your new housekeeper will help you with your garden."

Jake scowled. "I'm expected to find someone who'll take on gardening responsibilities in addition to housekeeping, cooking, and caring for Nikki? Just where do you think I'm going to find this paragon of domesticity?"

Sarah leveled a gaze at him that was maddeningly calm. "Tending the garden should only take a few minutes a week. But if your housekeeper isn't willing or able to do it, I'll be happy to come on weekends."

"See, Daddy?" Nikki said cheerfully. "I tol' you Miz Sarah would help."

Just what he needed—something to make this infuriatingly kind, considerate woman keep coming around after he finally got her out of his house. If she kept showing up, how was he supposed to ever get her out of his thoughts? She'd been stuck in his mind like a burr on a sheepdog ever since that blasted kiss.

But that was his fault—not Sarah's. And it was his problem—not Nikki's.

The thought hit him like a fist in the gut, knocking the wind out of him.

Hell. He'd been the one to initiate that confounded kiss, and he had no business blaming Sarah for it. He'd been behaving like a jerk ever since it happened—ignoring her, avoiding her, acting taciturn and surly. Instead of showing gratitude for the terrific job she was doing with Nikki and the house, he'd been trying to punish her.

For what?

For making herself indispensable. For being so wonderful with Nikki. For being warm and kind and...desirable.

Guilt gnawed at his belly. He needed to do an about-face, and he needed to do it fast. He had no right to treat her rudely just because he was having trouble keeping his distance from her. And he had no right to take out his frustrations over his insane attraction to her by depriving his daughter of a garden.

He raked a hand through his hair and heaved an exasperated sigh. "We'll work something out," he muttered. "I guess a garden isn't such a bad idea at that."

Nikki beamed, then smeared another streak of mud across her forehead as she brushed a strand of hair from her eyes.

Jake reached out and rumpled the child's feather-soft mop of curls, grateful for the opening she'd just given him to change the topic. "Looks like you need a haircut, sport." He glanced at Sarah. "Any idea where we can get that done around here?"

"There's a beauty shop in town. I can take her this afternoon, if you like. I need to go into town anyway to get a few groceries, and I thought I'd pick up some wallpaper samples for your master bath while I was at it."

"Fine." Getting Sarah off the ranch for a couple of hours sounded like a great idea, Jake mused. Now, if only he could only figure out a way to get her off his mind, as well.

"Wait'll Daddy sees our matchin' hairdos!" Nikki exclaimed. "Boy, will he be surprised!"

No more surprised than I am, Sarah thought, pulling the car to a stop in front of the house and fingering her new set of bangs.

She still didn't quite know how it had happened. The hairdresser had commented that a longer version of Nikki's slightly layered haircut would look good on Sarah, and the next thing she knew, she was in a chair, getting her hair cut, too.

She didn't know what had come over her. She'd been seized by an unaccustomed impulsiveness and she'd acted on it without thinking.

But now she was racked by second thoughts. Sarah peered at her reflection in the rearview mirror, not quite sure what to make of the woman staring back. Amazing how a hairstyle could make a person look so different, Sarah noticed. The bangs seemed to actually change the shape of her face. She looked younger, more carefree, less structured. Funny—she felt that way, too. She wondered what Jake would think of her new look.

Panic tightened her stomach as another thought struck her. *Oh dear, would he think she'd done it to impress him? Oh, dear. Had she?*

Of course not, she reassured herself, climbing out of the car to lug in the groceries and wallpaper books. His opinion meant absolutely nothing to her.

But her heart caught in her throat all the same when Jake strode into the kitchen as she was putting the groceries away. It stopped beating altogether when he stopped dead in his tracks and stared at her.

"See, Daddy?" Nikki bubbled. "I tol' you Miz Sarah's hair looks jus' like mine!"

"You changed your hair," he said unnecessarily, still transfixed.

"Do you like it?" The words were uttered before she could stop them from coming out of her mouth. Horrified, she turned her back, opened the refrigerator, and jabbed the bunch of celery in her hand into the vegetable bin. She wished she could put her head there, as well; after a dumb question like that, the vegetable bin was where it belonged.

Deliberately stalling, she spent several moments rearranging the jars on the lower refrigerator shelf.

When she finally slammed the door and turned around, he was still standing there, his dark eyes fixed on her face. "As a matter of fact, I like it a lot."

His voice had a low, unfamiliar timbre. She risked a

glance up, and something in his eyes made her pulse throb in her temple.

"I, uh, thought it would be easier to work with, not having to mess with barrettes and all." She couldn't stand the thought of him thinking she'd done it for him—even if she had.

Had she?

No. Of course not. She knew better than to try to change herself into something she wasn't. It was futile. It would be even more futile to try to change to please a man like Jake.

She self-consciously ran her fingers through her hair. "I, uh, needed a trim, and the hairdresser suggested bangs like Nikki's, so I thought I might as well try it...." She was babbling, giving him many more details than he could possibly want. Why was she carrying on at such length? Why couldn't she just shut up?

She ducked her head and blindly yanked items from the grocery bag, driven by a strange compulsion to defend her actions. "It can actually be a good idea to try something new from time to time, so..."

"You look real pretty."

She froze; her face turned as red as the picture on the label of the canned tomatoes she was holding. The next second, she whipped around toward the pantry, but not before he'd seen her eyes light up like a kid's on Christmas morning.

Something stirred in Jake's chest. He'd never known a woman to get such wholehearted pleasure from such a simple compliment. Was she really so unaccustomed to flattery? He recalled what she'd told him about her mother's criticisms and he wondered.

He remembered that she'd mentioned a former fiancé and he wondered some more.

One thing he didn't have to wonder about—he knew for a fact that he liked putting that look on her face a whole lot more than he liked being responsible for the tense frown she usually adopted every time he entered the room. He'd spent the afternoon regretting his curt behavior toward her and trying to think of ways to make it up to her.

He was struck with a sudden inspiration. He nudged Nikki. "I've got a great idea. Why don't I take you two glamour gals out to dinner tonight? Miss Sarah is due for a night off."

The child jumped up and down excitedly. "Can we go for pizza?"

"I was thinking about the steakhouse we passed on the highway. I don't remember the name of it."

"Freddie's," Sarah supplied.

"That's it. What do you say?"

"Do they have kid's meals?" Nikki asked.

"I'm sure they have something you'd like."

Sarah regarded him hesitantly. "You two go ahead. I'll stay here."

Oh, no, Jake thought. She wasn't about to duck out of this the way she'd been ducking him all week. He was determined to make amends for his behavior, and she wasn't going to stop him.

Besides, he had her over a barrel. "You can't. The doctor won't let me drive yet."

Thirty minutes later, they all piled into the cab of the pickup. Sarah had changed into a loose blue cotton dress that flattered her eyes, and Nikki was wearing a bow in her freshly trimmed hair. The child jabbered happily all the way to the restaurant and kept up a steady patter throughout the meal. Jake was glad most of Nikki's remarks didn't require a reply, because he was having a hard time following the conversation. He was too busy watching Sarah.

He liked the way she encouraged Nikki to use polite table manners without scolding. He liked the way she laughed at his jokes. He liked the way she unconsciously kept fiddling with her new bangs. He liked the way she held her fork and how her lips closed around it when she took delicate little bites of her steak and potato.

Hell, he liked everything about her. She'd gone out of her way to help him out of a bad situation, and he'd acted like a first-rate ingrate. He owed her an apology.

He found his chance to make one later that evening when they stepped into the hall together after putting Nikki to bed.

Their eyes met, and a charge of electricity surged through him. He saw Sarah's pupils dilate before she glanced away.

She nervously fingered her dress. "Thanks for dinner."

He gave a wry smile. "I owe you a lot more than dinner. You've been a real lifesaver since we moved here. I realize I haven't been the easiest person to deal with, and I want to apologize for that."

Sarah's eyes were soft and forgiving. "Nobody's at their best when they don't feel well."

He appreciated the way she was letting him off the hook so easily. Most women he knew would hold his admission of bad behavior over him for months, only lowering it occasionally to bash him over the head with it. "Well, I haven't been much help getting things settled around the house. I've been pretty busy trying to get the ranch up and running. Is there anything you need for me to do? Put up shelves or window shades or anything?"

After a moment of surprised silence, Sarah smiled. "As a matter of fact, there is something. I went ahead and ordered wallpaper for the kitchen and Nikki's room, but I need you to select something for the master bedroom. I have no idea about your tastes, and a bedroom is so personal...." Her voice trailed off weakly, as if she found the topic embarrassing. "Anyway, I've got some sample books in the kitchen."

Jeezum Pete, she was blushing. She really was an innocent, Jake thought, oddly pleased by the fact. He tilted his head toward the kitchen. "Let's go take a look."

They settled side by side at the oak table, a large book spread in front of them. Jake would have preferred to study

Sarah's face instead of pages of stripes and plaids and squiggles, but he forced himself to pay attention as she opened the cover. "I don't know what colors or kinds of patterns you like."

JaKe thumbed through the pages. The assortment was mind-boggling. "I can't picture any of these covering a whole wall. What do you suggest?"

"Well, maybe you should start by selecting a color."

"I like lots of colors."

"Let's narrow it down. What color makes you feel good?"

The color of your eyes. Criminy, he couldn't very well say that. Jake shifted uneasily in his chair and searched his mind for another answer.

Sarah read his hesitation as indecision. "Is there a color that has good memories associated with it?"

Yeah. The color of your lips.

"Maybe you should pick one that reminds you of someone. What was your wife's favorite color?"

The mention of Clarissa hit him like a bucket of cold water. He propped his forearms on the table and scowled. "Damned if I know. But if I did, it'd be the last color I'd pick."

Sarah's eyes grew troubled. "Oh...I'm so sorry. I know how much you loved her and how much you miss her and all. I just thought her favorite color might comfort you. I didn't think about the memory being painful." She leaned forward and covered his hand with hers. Her palm was as soft as suede. "I'm so sorry," she murmured.

Damn. Her sympathy made him feel like a fraud.

Jake abruptly scooted back from the table, his chair screeching on the hardwood floor. He raked his hand through his hair and rose. "You've got it all wrong about how things were between my wife and me."

Her eyes widened in confusion. He lumbered to the hallway and looked out, making sure they were alone, then stalked back, his lips tight. "I don't want Nikki to know.

She was too young to remember anything, and I want her to think the best of her mother.''

"Don't want her to know what?''

"What I'm about to tell you.'' Memories, coarse and unpleasant as a wet horsehair blanket, pressed on him so heavily he thought he might smother under the weight. He drew a deep breath. "Clarissa and I didn't have the made-in-heaven marriage you seem to think we had. I married her because I got her pregnant, not because I loved her. I'm ashamed to say I didn't even know her very well. Anyway, I tried to make the best of it. I did my damnedest to make her happy. I've always figured the best thing two parents can do for a child is to have a stable marriage, so I tried. Believe me, I tried.''

Jake jammed his hands into his pockets and began pacing, his limp more pronounced than it had been all day. He didn't care that his leg hurt. He almost welcomed the pain as a diversion from the pressure he felt inside. "Nothing worked. I think she hated me for getting her pregnant. She was bored and restless and unhappy. After Nikki was born, she was more interested in getting her figure back than in caring for the baby. She resented Nikki for tying her down.''

Sarah stared at him, her lips parted.

Jake swallowed back the bitter taste in his mouth. Blowing out a harsh breath, he leaned against the kitchen sink. "She died in a plane crash with my best friend. He was a crop duster. Their plane went down right after take-off.'' Jake's throat was dry and felt like it was starting to close up. "I had to go identify the bodies. It was the most horrible day of my life. Through it all, I kept wondering what she was doing in that plane.''

Jake stopped, unsure he could continue. But the pressure inside him demanded release, and it urged him on.

He grabbed a glass from the cabinet, splashed in some tap water and drained it, then turned back around. "When I got home that night, I found out. A Dear John letter was propped on my pillow. Clarissa was leaving me for my best friend. And it wasn't just me she was leaving. She was leaving Nikki behind, too.''

"Oh, Jake." Sarah's hand was at her mouth, her voice little more than a whisper.

A nerve twitched in Jake's jaw. "So now you know. Everyone back home knew, too. That was the main reason I moved away. Nikki was getting to an age when I was afraid she'd start hearing the rumors.''

Sarah's face was awash in emotion. She wore her feelings on her sleeve, and right now she looked just like he felt.

She rose and went to him, her eyes filled with tears. Her hand was warm on his upper arm. "How could she do that?" she whispered. "Nikki was just a baby."

His hands clenched and unclenched at his sides. "I've asked myself the same thing a million times. The only thing I've wondered about more was if there was anything I could have done to prevent it."

Sarah reached out her other hand and touched his hair, stroking it as if he were a hurt child. She was standing so close he could feel the heat of her body, or at least he imagined he could. Her nearness eased the tight, heavy feeling binding his chest.

"Surely you're not blaming yourself," she said softly.

Jake stared at the far wall and shrugged.

"You shouldn't. You can't." Her voice was low, her tone sure and firm. Her hand on his hair was soothing, almost hypnotic. He stood perfectly still, not wanting her to stop. "Nikki showed me her picture. She was very beautiful."

In her own gentle way, Sarah was offering him an excuse for the one thing he'd lambasted himself for the most—ever getting involved with a woman as shallow as Clarissa in the first place. In his own mind, it was just further proof that he was relationship-impaired.

Not that he completely regretted their involvement, he

reminded himself. Nikki was worth every miserable moment he'd ever endured at Clarissa's hands.

But he wasn't willing to do it again. He wasn't willing to risk ever making another woman as unhappy as he'd made Clarissa.

Clarissa. A mental picture of her washed through his mind like battery acid. Jake drew back, blew his breath through his teeth and studied a patch of peeling wallpaper.

"What was she like?" Sarah asked softly.

Jake kept his gaze on the wall, his mind playing a videotape of memories. "Well, like you said, she was beautiful. And if she put her mind to it, she could be charming. But underneath it all, she was self-absorbed. And childish. And narcissistic."

He looked at Sarah, then found he couldn't look away. Her eyes were a place of solace. Behind the lenses of her glasses, her eyes radiated warmth like a fire burning behind a glass fireplace screen, beckoning and drawing him in. He stood there, gazing at her, and felt a longing for something he couldn't name.

"She was cold. She wasn't anything like you."

The sympathy in Sarah's eyes blazed into something else. She was standing so close he could see the facets of her irises, see where the gray melted into dark blue around her pupils.

He couldn't breathe. He couldn't think. He only knew he had to get closer. He craved her the way an alcoholic would crave a drink. He wanted to see her as God had made her—with no barriers between them, with nothing distancing her from him.

He reached out and took off her glasses.

He heard her sharp intake of breath. "Can you still see me?" he asked.

She nodded. "I...I'm nearsighted. I can see things close up without my glasses, but I have trouble seeing at a distance." Her voice was weak and wobbly, and she took a shaky step back.

"Then you shouldn't get too far away." He pulled her closer. One of his hands delved into the thick silk of her hair and slipped through the strands to cradle her face. "You have the most beautiful eyes I've ever seen." He traced a thumb along one of her eyebrows. "So kind and warm and giving..."

His hand slipped down to her cheek. Her skin felt as soft as it looked, like the underside of a rose petal. The warmth in her eyes grew, heating the air between them until something flared and pulsed to life.

He wanted to kiss her so badly he ached. He stared at her lips the way a starving man might stare at a plate of ribs.

But oh, dear God, he didn't want to hurt her. He knew in his heart that he would if he kissed her again, because he wouldn't want to stop. Just the memory of her sweet, hot responsiveness made him throb for more.

He knew he'd better call a halt now, while he still had a modicum of self-control left. With an effort, he backed away. But he couldn't turn away from that wanting look in her eyes.

Criminy. He ran a hand down his face. Maybe the best thing to do was level with her. He drew a deep breath. "I want you, Sarah. I want to pick you up and carry you off to my bedroom and make love to you all night."

Her eyes were smoky and passion-glazed, and he was sorely tempted to stop talking and act on his words. He forced himself to continue, his voice thick and rough. "But I don't believe in love and marriage, and you're the kind of woman who won't be happy with anything less. I've never seen a successful marriage up close, but I've seen several bad ones. Believe me, there's nothing worse. I won't go through it again. I won't put another woman through it. And I won't put Nikki through it."

Sarah's expressive eyes were talking to him, and the message he heard was ripping his resolve to shreds. *I don't care. Just love me tonight.*

Well, she *would* care, he told himself vehemently. She would care plenty in the morning. She wasn't the type of woman who would take lovemaking lightly. And he wasn't going to kid himself; there was no way he could make love to Sarah without getting in a whole lot deeper than he ever intended.

Hell, he was in over his head now, just having this conversation with her.

His hands slid from her face to her shoulders, then trailed down her arms. Reluctantly, he released her. "You deserve a man who can love you with his whole heart, and I don't have a whole heart to give, Sarah." He stared at her, fighting the temptation to pull her back into his arms and kiss her halfway into tomorrow. He swallowed hard. "Well, now you know where things stand. I think I'd better go to my room before I do something both of us will end up regretting." He pushed away from the counter and strode out of the room.

Sarah watched him go, her knees weak, her heart pounding so hard it felt like it would bound out of her chest. She made her way back to the table and sank into a chair, her head reeling with everything he'd told her.

But most of all, three words ricocheted through her mind, over and over again.

I want you. The very thought sent a thrill chasing through her, rippling from her toes to the ends of her hair.

I want you, too, Jake, her heart called after him.

No man had ever told her he wanted her, had ever made her feel this womanly or sexy or desirable. Jake had made her feel all that, and more.

He'd made her feel special. First-rate. Second to no one.

I want you, he'd said. He hadn't ended the kiss earlier in the week because he found her undesirable, she thought wonderingly. She hadn't been imagining the looks and glances and undercurrents between them.

I want you. Did he have any idea how those three little words would stand her world on end?

She ran a hand through her hair, trying to sort out her thoughts and her high-flying emotions, pondering all that he'd told her.

He wasn't still in love with his wife. He hadn't had the made-in-heaven marriage she'd envisioned. Just the opposite; it sounded like he'd had the marriage from hell. From what he'd told her, the union probably had been doomed from the beginning by Clarissa's immaturity and self-centeredness.

But he'd tried to make the best of it. He'd done the honorable thing. He'd put Nikki's well-being ahead of his own happiness. He'd struggled to make the marriage work.

He was a good man with a good heart—in spite of his too-handsome-to-be-a-decent-person appearance. The thought softened and expanded inside her like a seed that had been germinating for some time but was only now erupting through the soil. Sarah's hand fluttered to her chest, where her heart felt tender and swollen with emotion.

Jake's own heart was bitter, she reflected. She'd almost been able to taste it as he'd talked about his marriage. And it was no wonder; he'd been betrayed by his wife as well as his best friend. Given that fact, along with his bad experiences as a child, she could see why he was so determined to avoid involvement.

But his eyes had looked so sad, so lonely, so full of pain when he'd talked about his marriage that she'd thought her heart would break. For a man as restrained and reserved as Jake, telling her the truth about his wife must have been as intimate an act as lovemaking.

A shiver chased up her arms. Jake might not have made love to her tonight, but he'd gotten inside her all the same.

Her thoughts swam like jumbled letters in a bowl of alphabet soup, clustering and sorting to form just three words.

I want you.

Sarah sat at the kitchen table and pressed those words to her heart, unwilling to leave the room where they'd been spoken, until the hour grew late and the rising moon spilled its light through the window.

Chapter Seven

Sarah gingerly placed the contact lens in her eye, then stood back and blinked. Her vision cleared as she scrutinized her reflection in the bathroom mirror.

She squinted, then blinked again. With her new haircut and no glasses, she didn't look like herself at all.

She didn't feel like herself, either, she thought, running a comb through her bangs. The episode with Jake last night had set her normal view of herself on its ear.

He found her desirable. The realization sent a shiver running through her body. The most desirable man she'd ever met had said he wanted *her*. It was all too incredible to absorb.

The thrilling concept had kept her awake for most of the night. Unable to sleep, she'd gotten up around midnight and driven to her little house in town. Once there, she'd grabbed some clothes from her closet, gathered up a long-abandoned box of cosmetics her mother had sent, snatched up her contact-lens case and solutions, and driven back to Jake's ranch with some fuzzy, half-formed notion of irresistibly transforming herself.

She'd nearly chickened out this morning. Correction, she chided herself, switching off the bathroom light. She *had* chickened out—on everything except the lenses. She was wearing her baggiest shirt and most shapeless pair of jeans, and hadn't had the nerve to even think about makeup.

She headed to the kitchen, giving herself a silent pep talk to bolster her flagging confidence. There was no reason not to wear her contacts. She'd bought them long before she'd ever met Jake Masters, and she could actually see better with them than she could with her glasses. Not to mention the fact that they were more practical for working with young children, who were often inclined to yank her glasses off her nose, she thought defensively.

She had every right to wear them this morning. There was no reason at all for her to feel nervous about it.

No reason at all, except for everything that had happened last night.

Sarah froze in the kitchen doorway, stricken by a sudden attack of panic.

Oh, dear. What on earth had she been thinking? She needed her glasses. They made her feel safe, they shielded her, they somehow kept the world at bay. Most important, they kept her from feeling like she was trying to be attractive. If she wasn't trying, she couldn't be failing.

She couldn't face Jake without them. She must have suffered temporary insanity. She turned, ready to race back to her room, and bumped solidly into Jake.

He caught her by the shoulders. "Sorry. Are you okay?"

All of her senses scattered. It took her a moment to collect her thoughts enough to nod.

He stared at her, and she felt her face color. Without her glasses, she felt naked. Exposed. Vulnerable.

And her contact-lens-enhanced vision made it all too clear that he was flat-out, drop-dead gorgeous. She swallowed, her mouth suddenly dry, and tried to avert her eyes, but his face drew her gaze like a magnet.

His brow knitted in concern. "Couldn't you find your glasses? I think I left them on the counter."

"On the counter?" she echoed vaguely, lost in her study of his features. She was close enough to see the individual whiskers on his jaw, the separate hairs of his eyebrows.

He shifted uneasily. "Yeah. I'll go look." He dropped his hands and strode into the kitchen.

"I, um, didn't lose them," she called after him.

He turned around, surprised. "No?"

"No. I'm…I'm wearing contacts."

His eyebrows lifted in surprise. "I didn't know you had contacts."

"I've had them for about a year." Sarah's face turned even redder. No telling what implications he was reading into the fact that she'd shown up wearing them this morning. She struggled to come up with a plausible explanation. "My, uh, glasses are getting loose—they keep sliding down my nose. I need to get them refitted, I guess." Oh, heavens—couldn't she come up with something better than that? As excuses went, that one was lamer than a three-legged dog.

"You look real nice."

Pleasure poured over her like bathwater over Nikki's rubber duck. Not wanting him to see how his remark had affected her, she dipped her head and scooted into the kitchen. "I'll make your breakfast. You must be starved."

"Actually, I already ate."

Sarah's eyebrows flew up. "But it's not even six in the morning! And it's a Sunday."

Jake shrugged. "I'm an early riser." No point in telling her he'd been up most of the night, too aroused to sleep.

He flung open a low cabinet and pulled out an iron skillet. "Nikki's up early, too. She's playing school with her dolls in her room. I was just getting ready to fix her some scrambled eggs. Would you like some?"

"Oh, let me do that," she said quickly, reaching for the pan. "That's my job."

He jerked it away. "I like to cook when I have the time." Besides, if he was busy cooking, maybe he could avoid staring at her.

He pulled a carton of eggs from the refrigerator, along with a gallon of milk and the butter dish, then closed the refrigerator door with his elbow. "I usually make breakfast on Sundays, anyway. That was always the day our housekeeper took off." He glanced over at her. "Now that I'm able to maneuver around the house, you ought to take the day off as well."

If he got her out of the house, maybe he could curb his raging libido. He had no intention of getting seriously involved with anyone, and he knew he couldn't get physically involved with Sarah without an emotional component entering into it. All the same, having her around posed a serious temptation.

He'd told her as much last night, he thought, opening a drawer to extract a fork to mix the eggs. So why the heck did she show up wearing contacts this morning? Hell, if he didn't know better, he would think she was trying to seduce him.

The thought made him freeze—just as the drawer slammed shut on his index finger.

"Oww!" Pain shot through his finger. He extricated his hand from the drawer and shook it in the air, biting his lower lip to keep from cursing aloud.

Sarah immediately stepped up and took a look at his hand, her brow creased with concern. "I'll get some ice."

"What's wrong, Daddy?" Nikki stood in the doorway, her cherubic face scrunched into a worried frown.

"Slammed my finger in the drawer."

"Why'd you do that?"

Because this confounded woman has my head spinning till I can't think straight. He gritted his teeth. "It was an accident. It'll be okay in a moment."

"Why don' you ask Miz Sarah to kiss it? It always makes my boo-boos better if she kisses me where it hurts."

If Sarah kissed him where he really needed it, he would be in a whole lot worse shape than he was now. It was thoughts like those that had him so sleep-deprived he'd slammed his hand in the drawer in the first place.

Sarah handed him a plastic sandwich bag filled with ice. He wrapped it around his finger, thinking of another part of his anatomy that could benefit from an ice pack as well.

"Thanks," he grunted. He turned to Nikki, who was still eyeing him with concern. "I'm okay now," he reassured her.

"I knew Miz Sarah would make it better," the child said solemnly. She peered at Sarah. "Hey, you're not wearin' your glasses!"

"I know. I'm wearing contact lenses."

"What are contack lizzes?"

Sarah grinned at the child. "They're tiny round discs that fit right in my eyes and help me see better."

"Do they hurt?"

"No. They were fitted by a doctor, so they don't."

"Oh. Well, you look pretty. Are you goin' somewhere special?"

"I, uh…" Sarah hesitated. "Well, actually, I thought I might go to church."

"Can Daddy and I go, too?" Nikki asked eagerly. "We used to go to church. I always got to wear frilly dresses. But we haven't gone in a long time."

Jake shifted guiltily. He'd stopped taking her to church back home because the local gossip had gotten to be too much to bear. Now that they'd moved, he had no excuse not to find a good church and start attending regularly.

He wasn't stuck on any particular denomination. Whatever church Sarah went to must be a good one, if she was an example of it. She was the kind of woman he hoped Nikki would grow up to be—kind, gentle, capable, compassionate.

Hell, it wouldn't hurt him to spend a little time in church, either, considering the direction his thoughts had been taking lately. Besides, a nice, bland outing with Sarah might do him a world of good. Maybe it would normalize things between them, help put out the fire that raged inside him every time he got within fifty paces of her. Avoiding her sure hadn't worked; the only thing it had accomplished was to make him feel like a jerk. It hadn't diminished the strange fascination she held for him in the least.

Perhaps overexposure was the key. If he had enough safe, non-romantic, everyday encounters with her, maybe the newness would wear off, she would lose her appeal, and he could go about his business, same as usual.

He pulled the ice bag off his finger. "Going to church sounds like a good idea. If you don't mind taking us with you, that is."

"Oh, I don't mind. I don't mind at all." A little thrill raced through Sarah, immediately followed by an attack of anxiety.

Oh, dear. She hadn't really planned on going to church at all. She'd just said the first thing that had popped into her head because she hadn't wanted Jake to think she'd worn the contacts on his account.

What on earth would she wear? People dressed up on Sundays in Oak Grove, and the only nice outfits she'd brought to the ranch were the dress she'd worn last night and a dress her mother had sent for her birthday—a hot-pink number far shorter, brighter and tighter than anything she would normally ever wear. She'd snatched it out of her closet at home last night when she'd been floating on that fluffy cloud—the one that had surrounded her ever since Jake had said he wanted her.

He wanted her. The thought made her hot and cold all over again, sending thrills chasing up and down her spine like a soprano practicing scales.

Why not wear the dress? Sarah asked herself with an unfamiliar recklessness. Just because it wasn't her usual style didn't mean there was anything wrong with it. The neckline was scooped, but it wasn't indecently low. The hemline was short, but it wasn't overly revealing. The fit was snug, but it wasn't distasteful.

There was nothing offensive about the dress. It wasn't at all inappropriate for church.

It was just inappropriate for her personality.

Or was it? she wondered. She felt brand-new on the inside, now that she knew Jake found her attractive. Maybe she should try some new things on the outside, as well.

She turned away and pulled some silverware out of the drawer, trying her best to act casual, not wanting her quaking nerves to show. "We've got plenty of time to make the early service," she said in what she hoped passed as a normal voice. "Nikki, why don't you help me set the table?"

Jake looked around uneasily as he rose with the rest of the congregation for the closing hymn. Two blue-haired old women in the next row stared openly at him, and a family across the aisle turned and waved.

Sarah smiled and waved back. Jake was acutely aware of her beside him, wearing an eye-popping pink dress that showed off a set of curves lusher than anything he'd ever imagined.

If he'd thought coming to church with Sarah would neutralize the way he felt around her, he was sorely mistaken. Of course, he hadn't known he would be left alone with her when Nikki happily trotted off to children's church with the rest of the preschoolers. And he sure hadn't figured that the entire congregation would be viewing them with such undisguised interest, either.

Sarah opened a hymnal and held it out for him to share. Reluctantly, he stepped closer to hold half of the book. Just as he'd feared, the scent of her soft, flowery perfume wafted over the pages to mercilessly tantalize him. Even worse, his position beside her afforded him a knee-weakening view down her neckline. From any other angle, her dress was perfectly respectable, but from this vantage point, it was practically X-rated. Despite his best efforts, he couldn't keep his eyes on the lyrics to "All Things Bright and Beautiful" because they kept focusing on the bright, beautiful sight of Sarah's breasts.

With a scowl, Jake looked ahead to the altar. This wasn't working. Not at all. Instead of subduing his feelings for her, this was simply intensifying them—and making the two of them a subject of public speculation, to boot. Judging by the number of sidelong glances thrown their way throughout the service, the nature of their relationship was going to be a hot topic at Sunday dinners all around town.

He'd been surprised at how many people had greeted Sarah as they'd entered the church. She not only seemed to know everyone in Oak Grove but she also seemed to have taken care of most of them in one capacity or another. One woman had thanked her for sending a casserole when she was ill, another had expressed her appreciation for sewing her child's costume for a school play, and yet another had promised to repay her as soon as she found employment for providing free day-care while she job hunted.

Sarah wasn't just his personal angel of mercy. She was Mary Poppins to the whole danged town.

The realization irritated the hell out of him, and it irritated him even further that he didn't know why. It just didn't seem right that so many people should be taking advantage of her kindly nature, he rationalized. It didn't seem right that she should spend so much time and energy on the needs of others.

It didn't seem right that her acts of kindness weren't exclusive to him.

Jake scowled, displeased by the proprietary nature of his thoughts. What ever happened to familiarity breeding contempt? Instead of losing her appeal, she was rapidly gaining more than ever. The more he learned about her, the more he found to love about her.

Love? The thought jarred him so that he nearly dropped the hymnal. *What in blue thunder was he thinking?*

He didn't mean it literally, he reassured himself. It was merely a figure of speech—like saying he loved barbecue or football or Quarter horses.

Or silky-haired brunettes with soft gray eyes and groin-tightening curves, his mind taunted.

Hell. Jake ran a finger under the knot of his tie. Just because he liked certain things about her didn't mean he was in love with her. He didn't think he had the capacity to love a woman. In any event, he never intended to get close enough to one to find out.

"Jake?"

Sarah's voice jerked him back to the present, and he abruptly realized that the hymn had ended and everyone else had already filed out of the pew.

"We need to go get Nikki."

"Yeah. Okay," he said gruffly, edging into the aisle.

"Why, hello there, Sarah...Jake!"

Deb's round, kindly face beamed at them from the end of the pew. In spite of his foul mood, Jake smiled back as she introduced her husband, Harry, a tall man with a friendly handshake who kept his other arm firmly locked around his wife's ample waist.

"Sarah, you look wonderful!" the older woman exclaimed. "I love what you've done with your hair. And your dress is just beautiful!"

"Thanks." Sarah flushed under her friend's praise, feeling as though her motives were all too transparent.

"Doesn't she look marvelous in her contacts?" Deb asked Jake. "I'm always telling her she should wear them more often."

Knock it off, Deb, Sarah silently pleaded, mortified by her friend's attempt to wring a compliment from Jake.

Jake nodded, looking as uneasy as Sarah felt.

"You're looking good, too, Jake," Deb continued. "It's wonderful to see you up and around."

"It's great to be that way."

"I told you Sarah would take good care of you."

Jake gave Sarah an uneasy glance and shoved a hand in the pocket of his slacks. "And you were right. But you'll be glad to know you should have her back at the preschool soon. The ad for a housekeeper ran today, so hopefully I'll be hiring someone in a couple of days."

Sarah gazed at Jake, her spirits plummeting to the toes of her pumps. She'd known the ad was running soon, but she hadn't realized it was today.

That meant that in just a matter of days, she would have to move out of Jake's house and back into her own. Like Cinderella's when the clock struck midnight, her life was about to revert to the drab, colorless existence she'd led before she'd met Jake.

That was just what she'd been living, she thought suddenly—a fairy tale. But this one wasn't going to have a "happily ever after" ending. Jake had told her as much last night. She'd been so caught up in the amazing revelation that he found her desirable that she'd somehow failed to register the fact that he had no intention of ever acting on that attraction.

Sarah's chest constricted painfully. As soon as he hired a permanent housekeeper, she would be out of his house, out of his mind and out of his life. Her stay at his ranch might be the highlight of her entire life, but it was nothing more than a minor occurrence in his.

What a fool she was, she thought bitterly. In all likelihood, the only reason Jake felt any attraction to her in the first place was because she was plain enough to be safe. He could safely project his needs onto her because she didn't pose a real emotional threat.

All of her daydreams had been just that—dreams, and nothing more. Just the silly, pathetic dreams of a lonely spinster.

She swallowed hard, trying to choke back the tears that threatened her eyes. She suddenly felt ridiculous in the dress, naked without her glasses, and foolish for trying to improve her appearance. It was all pointless, all nothing but an exercise in futility.

The sooner she got her life back to normal, the easier it would be to accept it, she told herself. And for the sake of her pride, it was important that she initiate it.

She drew a deep breath. "I've been meaning to ask you, Jake, now that your leg is so much better, would it be all right if I start teaching half days at the preschool? Your house is all unpacked and settled, so there's really no need for me to be there while Nikki's at school."

Jake's eyebrows flew up in surprise.

"Now, Sarah, there's no hurry," Deb interjected, still in full matchmaker mode. "I've got everything completely under control at Happy Times."

"I'm sure you do, but I'm anxious to get back to work," Sarah said. "I've missed the children, and I've missed teaching. I'll still be able to watch Nikki, fix meals, and keep house."

Jake shoved his hands in his pockets. "Sounds like a lot to handle, but if that's what you want to do, it's fine with me."

"Great." Sarah forced a smile. "Well, we'd better go get Nikki. I'll see you tomorrow, Deb."

Sarah ducked her head as she hurried away, hoping neither of them noticed the suspicious way her eyes were brimming with moisture.

Chapter Eight

A loud scream jerked Sarah awake.

She groped on the nightstand for the alarm clock. Half past midnight. Foggy-headed, she sat up and reached for her glasses, not sure if she'd dreamed the noise or actually heard it. And then it sounded again—a terrified, high-pitched scream, curdling down the hallway.

Nikki. Her heart in her throat, Sarah threw off the covers, grabbed her robe from the end of the bed, and flew to the child's room.

She found the little girl huddled in her bed, her bedraggled teddy bear clutched to her chest, her eyes wide with fear.

Sarah crawled onto the bed and cradled the child against her. "Sweetheart, what's the matter?"

"A-a-a monster," the child babbled, burying her face against Sarah's breasts.

"Oh, honey, you've had a bad dream." Sarah rocked the child against her, her hands caressing her head.

"It seemed so r-r-real…" Nikki sobbed.

"What's the matter?"

Jake stood in the doorway, his hair rumpled, his chest bare, wearing a pair of jeans that were zipped but unbuttoned at the waist, as if he'd just hastily thrown them on. His brow was furrowed with concern, his jaw dark with unshaven stubble. Sarah's heart cartwheeled at the sight of him.

"Nikki had a bad dream."

"Aw, honey." The bedsprings creaked as he sat down on the other side of Nikki and took her in his arms. The sight of Nikki's soft blond curls against the thick mat of Jake's chest hair made Sarah's heart lurch. He held the child, stroking her back, until her sobs subsided.

"Do you want to talk about it?" he asked gently.

Nikki gave a loud sniffle. "It...it was a monster," she said solemnly. "An' it was chasing me. An' it was about to get me. An' I was scared!"

Jake's large, tanned hand sifted through Nikki's fine curly strands. Sarah watched, a lump forming in her throat.

"That sounds scary, all right." Jake gave her a tender smile. "Would it make you feel better if I check your room?"

Nikki nodded and snuggled against Sarah.

Jake crossed the room and opened the closet. "All right, all you monsters, time to come out!" he ordered.

Nikki giggled.

"I mean it, monsters," he boomed in an authoritative voice, giving the door a menacing glare. "Line up and file out, and make it snappy!"

Nikki laughed again.

"I've given you two warnings, and now I'm coming in after you!" Jake stormed into the closet and looked around. He stuck his head out the door, a look of mock surprise making his eyebrows rise comically. "Looks to me like they've already left."

Nikki giggled wildly. "There were never any monsters in there, Daddy!"

"Oh?" Jake rubbed his head, pretending to be confused,

as he exited the closet. "Well, how about behind the rocker?" He peered behind the chair in the corner with exaggerated care. "Hmm." He scratched his jaw thoughtfully, then held a finger in the air, his eyes open wide. "I've got it. They must be under your bed!"

"Nooooo!" Peals of delighted giggles erupted from the child. "Daddy's teasin'," Nikki told Sarah. "I like it when he does that."

Sarah tightened her arm around the child and smiled. She liked it, too. She liked it when he did other things, as well— like stalk around the room wearing only a pair of low-riding jeans. The fact of the matter, Sarah decided, was that she liked just about everything about him. At the moment, she was particularly taken with the way his biceps bulged every time he bent his arm, the way his sleep-tousled hair stuck out on one side, and how the springy, dark curls on his chest narrowed like the shaft of an arrow to point straight down into his jeans.

"We'd better check under the bed just to be sure. You'll have to help, though, Nikki. If I lift the bed skirt, will you look under it?"

With a nod, Nikki cheerfully bounded off the mattress, knelt down, and peered under the dust ruffle. "I tol' you Daddy," she said knowingly, sitting back on her heels "No monsters."

Jake's wide-eyed, openmouthed look of surprise made Sarah laugh out loud. "You mean they all sneaked out when we weren't looking?"

Grinning widely, Nikki put her hands on her waist. "It was just a dream, Daddy! There's no such thing as monsters."

"Oh." He rubbed his chin, pretending to digest this new bit of information. "Well, then, I guess that explains why we couldn't find any."

Nikki dissolved in a fit of giggles. Smiling broadly, Jake scooped her up, swung her around, then plopped her back on the bed.

"Think you can go back to sleep now?" he asked.

"Well...maybe after I have a drink of water. An' after you read me a book. An' after Miz Sarah tells me the princess story!"

Sarah met Jake's amused grin over the child's head. She smiled back, but her heart was strangely wistful. There was something so sweet about this moment; something so simple, yet so profound. It was a moment of perfect communication. One when they were so bound together by their love of Nikki that a simple glance could convey "Isn't she wonderful?" and "Isn't she exasperating?" all at the same time, along with "She thinks she's putting one over on us." and "I know it, but I'm going to let her get away with it anyway." and even, "I'm glad you're here to share this with me." All of that, communicated without a word spoken. It was the kind of silent, soul-mate exchange a husband and wife might share.

The longing in Sarah's chest tightened into a hard ache. What would it be like if that were the case—if Nikki were her child, if Jake were her husband? If the two of them were to tuck Nikki back in bed, walk down the hall to the master bedroom, and climb into that king-size bed together?

A shiver raced through her. She realized she was staring at Jake and was startled to discover that he was staring back, the look in his eye so heavy and intense, it felt like the weight of his hand.

His gaze roved over her. She was suddenly reminded that she was wearing nothing but a filmy pink gown edged in ridiculously delicate lace. Beautiful lingerie was her secret vice. She felt her face flame, embarrassed that he'd caught her wearing something so sheer and extravagant. She hoped he hadn't been able to see right through it. Even more, she hoped he didn't think it was foolish for a such a plain woman to wear something so lavish. "I...I'll go get the glass of water," she murmured, snatching up the matching robe and holding it in front of her like a shield as she fled down the hall to the bathroom.

She closed the door, turned on the faucet and splashed some water on her face, wishing it would cool her overheated thoughts. The sight of Jake, half dressed and fresh from his bed, was enough to unhinge any red-blooded woman, but the tender, funny way he'd comforted Nikki had caused her to have a complete meltdown.

With sudden clarity, she knew why. *She was in love with him.* She froze, still bent over the sink, water dripping from her face.

Dear heavens! She didn't want it to be true, but she couldn't deny that it was. Bits of evidence crowded into her mind, presenting her with an indisputable array of proof.

She'd started falling for him in that cow pasture, when his first coherent thought had been for Nikki. She'd grown to care for him even more as she'd come to realize he was more than a too-handsome-for-his-own-good hunk of brawn. He was smart. He was tender. He was hardworking. He was kind, and he had a great sense of humor. Last night, when he'd told her about his wife, she'd felt his pain so deeply her heart had ached. And when he'd said he wanted her, she'd never desired anything in her whole life as much as she'd yearned to make love with him at that moment.

As much as she wanted to make love with him right now.

Sarah abruptly shut off the water and reached for a towel. She couldn't allow herself to even think about it, she warned herself as she dried her face. He'd made it clear that he had no interest in a permanent relationship. He'd been badly burned by his first marriage, and his heart was deeply scarred.

Besides, he'd pointed out only yesterday that her role here was temporary. To start a romantic relationship destined to last a week or less would be foolish, pointless, and illogical.

But what good would logic do if it left her a dried-up old spinster who'd never known how it felt to love a man?

Her pulse throbbed in her throat as she stared, wide-eyed,

at her reflection in the mirror. This might be the only chance she would ever have in her life to discover how it could be between a man and a woman—to experience all the things that she'd dreamed about and wondered about and longed to share with a man she loved.

Jake had said he wanted to carry her off to his bed and make love to her all night long. Did she dare encourage him to act on those desires?

Her heart quickened at the thought. The question taunted her as she shrugged into her silk robe, filled a paper cup at the sink and carried it to Nikki's bedroom, where she found Jake reading the last page of a picture book. It continued to tease her as she recited the princess story, feeling Jake's eyes on her the whole time. It even flirted at the corners of her mind as she kissed the child good-night. But when she finally followed Jake into the hall and closed the door to Nikki's room behind her, she completely lost her nerve.

Jake stood in the shadows of the darkened hallway. She nervously tightened the sash of her robe and started to hurry past, but he stepped forward, blocking her way.

"Sorry your sleep was interrupted like that," he said. "Thanks for getting up to help calm Nikki down."

"Oh, I was glad to do it." Tongue-tied and awkward, Sarah fidgeted with the top of her robe. Now that she realized how strongly she felt about him, she didn't have a clue how to act around him. "I...I know how awful nightmares can be."

He eyed her curiously. "Sounds like the voice of personal experience. Do you have a lot of bad dreams?"

"Not anymore. But I used to."

"What about?"

"Snakes, mostly." She rubbed her hands along her upper arms and tried to suppress a shudder. "I hate the things." Uneasy with both the topic and Jake, she started to edge down the hall.

His hand suddenly shot out and caught her by the wrist.

He immediately released his hold, but her skin burned from the contact.

"I'm still too keyed up to sleep. Why don't we go fix some hot chocolate?"

Sarah hesitated.

"I hope you'll say yes, because I have no idea how to make the stuff. I probably won't be able to go to sleep without it."

He was gratified when she flashed one of her face-transforming smiles—the kind that seemed to light her up from the inside. "Okay."

Just as he'd figured—she was unable to refuse a request for help. Jake grinned as he followed her down the hall. He should be ashamed of himself for using such a deceptive ploy, but he'd suddenly been seized by a strange, strong reluctance to end the evening.

It was no wonder, he thought, eyeing her hungrily as she headed down the stairs and into the kitchen. She looked as delectable as a piece of cotton candy in that short pink robe with the sash cinched so tightly around her narrow waist. Until he'd seen her in that fitted dress, he'd had no idea she was hiding such a sweet little body under all those baggy clothes. Now that he did, he was having trouble thinking of anything else.

He swallowed hard as she bent to retrieve a pan from a low cabinet, causing the back of her robe to ride up provocatively high. Jumpin' Jehosophat, he thought, his mouth suddenly as dry as the Sahara. Her choice of nightwear was certainly a drastic departure from her taste in daytime fashion. He reached up to run a finger under a suddenly-too-tight collar, only to realize he wasn't wearing a shirt.

He ended up absently rubbing his chest as his eyes tracked her movements from the refrigerator to the stove. Did she normally wear lacy stuff like this under all that drab garb? And if so, for whose benefit was she wearing it?

The thought made him break into a sweat. He was suddenly brimming with questions about her. What was the full story of her breakup with her fiancé? Were there any men in her life now? She'd said she didn't have a love life, but that could just mean she was in the early stages of dating someone.

Maybe she'd even gone on a date this afternoon. She'd beat on a quick retreat after church, saying that since he'd given her the day off, she wanted to visit a friend in town.

Was the friend a man? The possibility made his stomach tighten into a hard knot. He needed to launch a fishing expedition to see if he could reel in some answers.

Jake leaned against the counter and watched Sarah turn on the burner. "Did you have a nice visit with your friend this afternoon?" he asked casually.

Sarah nodded.

"Anyone I know?"

"I don't believe so. Mrs. Milston is ninety-two years old and lives in the Oak Grove nursing home."

"Oh." Relief rolled through him. He searched for an innocuous remark to cover his inquisitiveness. "You seem to know everyone in town."

Sarah pulled a can of cocoa out of the cabinet. "Oak Grove is pretty small, and my grandmother was always active in the community. I used to visit her every summer, so everyone knows me through her."

"Did your fiancé ever come here with you?"

Sarah looked up, her gray eyes surprised. "No."

"Seems like you would have wanted him to meet your grandmother, since the two of you were so close."

Sarah hesitated a fraction too long. "She fell ill shortly after we got engaged. Dave couldn't tolerate sick people."

Nice guy, Jake thought sarcastically. He wondered how Sarah had been able to tolerate him.

"It was what broke us up," Sarah continued, measuring out some cocoa. "I wanted to move back here and take care of her, and he didn't want me to. He had our lives all mapped out—get married, buy a house in the suburbs, have two children exactly two years apart—and he didn't want anything to throw it out of kilter.''

"Sounds like a real control freak.''

"He was.''

"So what happened?''

Sarah shrugged. "I couldn't let Gran down. She was the only person who'd believed in me when I was going through those awful teen years, who helped me find other qualities to develop. She had stood up for me to Mom, and I wanted to return the favor. My folks were pressuring her to move, and I didn't want her to have to go to a nursing home.''

"So how did this Dave character take it?''

"Not well. He informed me that a woman like me wasn't likely to get another opportunity to marry a guy with so much to offer.'' Her mouth curved in a wry smile. "I told him I'd take my chances. I finally figured out that the only reason he was interested in me was because he needed someone to feel superior to.''

Jake felt his hackles rise. He should probably just let the subject drop, but a fierce sense of protectiveness propelled him to find out just how badly this creep had hurt her. "What did he mean, a woman like you? And why would this Mr. Wonderful of yours have any reason to feel superior to you?''

He watched her draw a shaky breath, saw her struggle to compose her face, and his heart squeezed tight in his chest.

Her hand shook as she stirred the milk. "Because of my appearance.''

The kitchen was suddenly as quiet as a confessional. The clock on the wall ticked loudly. Sarah's spoon scraped the bottom of the pan.

Jake felt like he was about to stumble into a land mine, but something inside urged him to press on. "What about it?''

Sarah wrapped her robe more tightly around her with one

hand and stirred the milk with the other, her eyes steadily fixed on the stove. "He was referring to the fact that I'm unattractive. 'A real Plain Jane' was the exact term he liked to use."

Anger ripped through Jake, filling him with adrenaline, tightening his muscles. If the dork thought Sarah was unattractive, he was an even bigger fool than he was a jackass. "What on earth did you ever see in this guy?"

Sarah's eyes didn't leave the milk. "I don't know. I guess I just figured beggars can't be choosers."

"And exactly what do you mean by that?"

Sarah lifted her shoulders. "I'm a realist. I knew I was going to have to put up with some major flaws in any man who'd want to marry me, because he'd be putting up with some major flaws in the way I look."

A fresh of surge of anger filled his veins. "Is that another thing Mr. Wonderful used to tell you?"

Sarah nodded, her hair obscuring her face.

"And you believed a jerk like that?"

Sarah shrugged, but her attempt to act nonchalant was ruined by the lone tear that slid down her cheek and hit the electric burner with a loud hiss. "He...he wasn't saying anything I didn't already know."

Jake studied her, his chest suddenly hot and tight. She'd told him about the confidence-destroying number her mother had worked on her, but he'd figured that was all part of an awkward-adolescent stage she'd outgrown. Had it damaged her self-image so badly that she'd almost married a man who would insult her to her face?

"You had no business being engaged to a low-life piece of scum like that. You deserve a whole lot better. Like I told you the other night, you need to hold out for someone who'll love you with their whole heart and soul." Jake scowled at her. "You don't have a clue how lovely you are, do you?"

"It's okay," she told him quietly. "I know what I look like."

The resignation in her voice made the taut spot in Jake explode like an overstretched hot-air balloon. "Evidently not. Sounds to me like your self-image is caught in some kind of teenage time-warp." He abruptly took her arm and pulled her away from the stove. "Come on."

Sarah found herself being firmly steered out of the kitchen. "Where are we going?" she asked in alarm as he led her down the hall.

"To my bedroom."

Before she knew what was happening, he'd propelled her up the stairs and into the master suite. Her eyes wide, her pulse pounding, she stared at his large rumpled bed. In all of her fantasies about coming here with Jake, she hadn't imagined it being anything like this.

A wave of panic washed over her. She balked, her knees quaking so hard she would have collapsed if he hadn't had such a firm grip on her arm. "Jake, I..."

"Come here," he urged, pulling her in front of him to stand before the full-length beveled mirror set in the door of his antique armoire. "Now take a look, and tell me what you see."

Sarah froze, her face burning with embarrassment.

Jake's hands squeezed her upper arms. "Go ahead. Describe what you see."

Sarah glanced at her reflection and cringed. "A tall, gawky woman with a homely face." She looked away, fixing her eyes on the tan carpet.

"That's not what I see," he said firmly. "Not at all." Moving his hands to her head, he tilted her face, forcing her to look straight into the mirror at her own reflection. Her heart began a rapid, unsteady staccato.

"I see a woman who got out of a warm bed because she heard a child cry. A woman who waited on me hand and foot while I was incapacitated, who put her own life on hold to come here and help me out because I didn't know a soul in town and couldn't take care of my daughter."

"That doesn't have anything to do with how I look," she whispered, her voice cracking.

"It damn sure does. You look like what you are—a kind, caring, beautiful woman. Maybe you're just not looking closely enough."

He urged her closer to the mirror, using his body to prod her forward, then slid both hands into her hair. The unexpected intimacy of the gesture made her gasp.

"Look at your hair, Sarah," he said gently. His mouth was near her ear, and the warmth of his breath sent goose bumps chasing up her arms. His hands wove into her hair, slowly sifting thick strands through his fingers. "It's like scented silk—soft and sweet-smelling. I've wanted to touch it like this ever since I first saw you."

His fingers whispered across her cheek, leaving a trail of warmth in their wake. She watched in the mirror, mesmerized, as if she were watching a stranger. "I've wanted to touch your skin, too," he murmured. "Your beautiful, velvety skin."

One of his hands slid up and pulled off her glasses. "Are you close enough to see your reflection without your glasses?"

Numbly, Sarah nodded.

"Good, because I want you to take a good look at your eyes." Slowly, languorously, he traced a fingertip along her eyebrow. "When I woke up in that cow pasture and looked into your eyes, I thought you were an angel."

Sarah's stomach did a funny little somersault. He pressed nearer, and Sarah felt the front of his hard thighs against the back of hers. Heat, sudden and achy, licked low in her belly.

"And your lips..." Jake's voice grew husky as his finger traced the outline of her mouth. She heard him swallow. "I can't stop thinking about your lips. Ever since I felt them on mine, I've wanted to..."

The heat inside her burst into flame as his finger touched the center of her lips. Instinctively she turned toward him.

With a groan, he hauled her against him, lowered his head and claimed her mouth with his own.

Sarah clung to him, one hand in his hair, the other around his back. Her world narrowed to the feel of his lips on hers, his body against her own. Her life compressed and contracted to nothing but the points of contact with Jake—his hands splayed across her back, his chest crushed against her breasts, his hungry, searching mouth on hers, and finally, filtering through everything else, the hard proof of his desire pressing against her belly.

He hadn't been mouthing empty words of consolation, she realized, a terrifying sense of wonder thrilling through her.

It was true. He wanted her.

He eased away just enough to cup her breast with his hand. She heard a moan and was shocked to realize it had come from her own throat. His thumb slowly rubbed across the taut, pebbled peak of her breast.

"I want to see you," he murmured. "All of you."

His voice was rough with desire, and the sound of it inflamed her further. If only he would keep stroking her like that, she would do anything, everything he wanted. Her bones seemed to have melted into liquid heat.

He tugged on the sash of her robe and eased it off. The air felt cool on her bare arms. She shivered against him and closed her eyes as he slipped the narrow straps of her gown off her shoulders. The gown slithered to the floor and pooled at her feet on top of the robe.

She was naked. Before the realization had time to fully strike home, Jake was holding her close. The thought that superseded all others was how delicious his chest felt against her breasts, how wonderful his fingers felt on her bare back.

"Sarah..." Her name came out as a long, guttural sigh. He turned her toward the mirror, cradling her back against him. His hot, rock-hard manhood burned against her through his jeans. "Sarah, just look at yourself."

She hesitated, fear nibbling at the edges of her consciousness. She didn't want to ruin this magical, wonderful spell he'd woven, didn't want to leave this incredible star-strewn place he'd taken her. If she opened her eyes, it might all disappear. She wanted to cling to the fantasy a little longer. He'd made her feel like a swan. She didn't want to look in the mirror and see an ugly duckling.

"Open your eyes," he urged softly. "I want you to see how beautiful you are."

Her heart raced and tripped, and the air in her lungs felt hot and heavy. Her breath came in short, shallow puffs. Slowly, slowly, she opened her eyes.

Dear heaven. The contrast of his brown, masculine fingers curling around her milky-white breast was shocking. Shocking, and powerful, and...extremely erotic.

Her gaze fastened on his face, and the hungry way his eyes glittered made her breath catch in her throat. He met her eyes in the mirror. "You're beautiful," he whispered.

And suddenly, she felt it. For the first time in her life, she truly felt beautiful.

She watched in the mirror, not daring to breathe, as he moved his hands across her, his lips murmuring words of praise. She felt like she was flying—as if she were having one of those out-of-body experiences she'd read about. But she couldn't be, she thought dazedly, because then she wouldn't be feeling the heavy warmth of his hands on her skin, the prickly stubble of his beard on her neck, the tantalizing heat of his breath against her ear.

She stood paralyzed, and suddenly she saw herself through his eyes. It was a revelation. She'd never thought of her body this way. She'd always considered her breasts too small, her waist too long, her hips too angular. She'd always dwelt on the negatives and had never really thought about her body's attributes—never thought of it as being so feminine, so touchable, so desirable, so...

"Beautiful," Jake breathed against her skin, his hand circling, stroking, teasing her breast.

"Beautiful here...and here." She watched, breathless, as his hand glided to her other breast. His mouth followed, nipping and kissing and stroking until her knees were weak with pleasure.

"And here." Both hands ran down her ribs, stopping at the indentation of her waist. His fingers spread wide as his hand dipped low across her belly. "And here."

Her knees shook and nearly buckled as his hands continued their erotic assault on her senses. She was quivering, burning, aching with need.

"I want you," he breathed against her ear. "I want to stretch you out and kiss every single, beautiful square inch of your—"

The blaring shriek of an alarm abruptly interrupted.

Jake jerked back. "What's that?"

"It...it sounds like the smoke detector." Sarah was suddenly aware of the faint but unmistakable smell of smoke. Her hand flew to her mouth. "Oh, my gosh...the pan of milk! We left it on the stove!"

Jake reached down, grabbed her nightclothes and glasses from the floor and thrust them at her. "I'll see to it. You go get Nikki and get out of the house."

He dashed from the room. Sarah struggled into her robe as she hurried toward the child's bedroom, her heart pounding, her head reeling, with one incongruent thought standing out clearly from the chaotic jumble in her mind: even in the face of the emergency, Jake's first act had been a considerate one—to hand her her clothes and glasses.

Thank goodness for smoke detectors, Jake thought, leaning against the barn door and watching Sarah's car send a cloud of dust into the sun-streaked air as she and Nikki drove off to preschool early the next morning. Last night's alarm had not only kept the house from burning down but had also prevented an entirely different type of conflagration.

He no more could have stopped himself from making

love to Sarah than he could have stopped a stampede of wild stallions with a butterfly net. And judging from the way Sarah had been responding to him, she'd had no inclination to stop, either.

Yes, sirree, it was a good thing that alarm had sounded when it did, before anything got burned besides the pan. And it was a good thing Sarah had awakened Nikki and hustled her out of the house, too. It might have been overly cautious, but the act had ensured that they had a pint-size chaperon when the crisis was over. He'd definitely felt in need of one. After Nikki had been tucked into bed for the third time that night, he'd gone directly to his room, closed the door firmly, and taken a long, cold shower.

He scuffed his boot in the dust of the barn floor. Not that the shower had helped any. Seeing Sarah naked, running his hands over her luscious body, kissing her flower-scented skin had started a fire inside him that mere water couldn't put out. Just thinking about it got him hot all over again.

Jake took off his Stetson and ran a hand through his hair. Despite his best intentions, he couldn't trust himself to keep his distance from her. Last night had been proof enough of that. All he'd intended to do was help her see how attractive she was. The next thing he knew, he'd been all over her like hide on a heifer.

At least his initial motives had been good, he told himself. He'd wanted to help her get over the harm that manipulative Dave character had inflicted on her already-damaged self-image. The jerk sounded like a first-class control freak—a weakling looking for someone weaker to keep under his thumb. Thank heavens, Sarah had had the pluck to stand up to him.

But all that was beside the point, because the situation between him and Sarah had become untenable. He couldn't trust himself to keep his distance, leaving only one solution: he had to get her out of his house. He needed to hire a new housekeeper, and he needed to do it fast. This week. Preferably today.

It was going to be impossible to find someone who measured up to Sarah, so there was no point in even trying. The first person he interviewed who didn't claim to converse with space aliens, have a serious personal hygiene problem, or seem to have connections with organized crime would get the job.

He slammed his hat on his head, pulled the barn door closed behind him and went in search of Buddy. He needed a ride back to the house. Now that Sarah had left to spend half the day at her preschool, he could finally work in his office on the mountain of paperwork that had accumulated over the past week while he'd tried to avoid being alone with her.

Besides, he wanted to be near a phone today so he could personally answer any calls generated by his newspaper ad. The sooner he got Sarah out of his house, the sooner he could get her off his mind—and away from the spot she was starting to occupy suspiciously close to his heart.

Chapter Nine

"**Y**ou seem pretty glum this morning," Deb remarked a week later, picking up the plastic tray of juice-filled paper cups in the preschool kitchen. "Got the back-at-work-full-time blues?"

Sarah screwed the lid on the gallon of apple juice, opened the refrigerator, and placed it on a low shelf. "I'm okay."

"You sure don't look it."

She sure didn't feel it, either. She'd moved out of Jake's house yesterday to make way for the new housekeeper, and she felt like the bottom had just dropped out of her world.

Deb's eyes were warm with sympathy. "Missing Jake and Nikki?"

Something awful. But she couldn't bring herself to admit it aloud. She was afraid to even confess the full extent of it to herself. Sarah forced herself to smile as she poured cheese crackers into paper muffin-liners for the children's midmorning snack. "Actually, I'm wondering where Nikki is. She's running late this morning."

"Do you think Jake will bring her?"

Sarah fervently hoped so. "I suppose so. I took him to his second follow-up appointment last Wednesday, and his doctor said he could start driving again."

It had been during the trip to the doctor's office that he'd told her he'd hired a permanent, live-in housekeeper. Mrs. Olsen had excellent credentials, he'd said; she'd been a professional full-time nanny in Shreveport, and she held a bachelor's degree in home economics. She was looking for a new position because the children she'd been caring for had outgrown the need for her services. She planned to move in Sunday afternoon.

Sarah had somehow mustered the wherewithal to congratulate Jake on finding such a well-qualified individual so quickly, even though her heart had been breaking. She'd secretly hoped Jake would realize he cared for her after what had happened between them the night of Nikki's nightmare. She was almost certain that he did; no one could have faked the tenderness and emotion he'd shown her that night.

But instead of a profession of love, all she'd gotten was another apology and the cold shoulder. He'd avoided her like the plague all week. True to what he'd told her, Jake was evidently bound and determined not to get involved.

It was probably a good thing she was moving out, Sarah had consoled herself. The longer she stayed, the more deeply attached she would grow. And the deeper her attachment, the harder it would be to leave in the long run.

In fact, she'd toyed with the idea of leaving right then and there, but she'd decided to remain for the rest of the week in order to supervise the team of painters and wallpaper hangers who were redecorating the house.

Sarah sighed as she stashed the half-empty bag of crackers in a cabinet. Who was she trying to kid? The truth was, she'd wanted to delay the inevitable for as long as possible.

When Jake had held her in front of that mirror and shown her how he saw her, he'd completely, utterly stolen her heart. It was as if he'd pulled a blindfold from her eyes.

He'd stripped away her cloak of self-loathing and helped her to see that she wasn't as hopelessly ugly as she'd always believed. He'd shown her, in fact, that parts of her were downright attractive—so attractive that he'd nearly made love to her despite all of his intentions not to get involved.

The thought sent a shiver up her spine.

How could she not love a man who'd helped her learn to love and accept herself? She might as well stay a few extra days, she'd figured. A broken heart could only hurt so much.

But "so much" could sure be a lot, Sarah realized now. After leaving the ranch yesterday, she'd spent one of the longest, loneliest, most miserable nights of her life at her little house. She didn't think of the place as home. Home wasn't an accurate term for a place where she felt so lonely.

The mention of Jake's name jerked her attention back to the present. "Jake's probably just running late," Deb was saying. "After all, he's got a new housekeeper to break in."

The bell over the door jangled, and Sarah looked up to see Nikki running toward her. Her heart pounding, she held out her arms to the child, all the while scanning the doorway for Jake's tall form. Instead of a handsome cowboy, however, a thin, tight-lipped woman in her mid-fifties marched behind the girl. "I'm Hannah Olsen," the woman announced. "I'm sorry we weren't more punctual, but the child's father insisted on letting her sleep late this morning."

Nikki threw herself into Sarah's arms. "Oh, Miz Sarah, I missed you so!" The little girl buried her face in Sarah's skirt and sobbed.

"Honey, what's the matter?" Sarah asked, full of concern.

"I can assure you that nothing in the world is the matter with any child in my care."

Sarah's spine immediately went rigid. There were few

things she hated more than hearing an adult deny or belittle a child's feelings. "She's obviously very upset about something," she told the woman, kneeling down in front of the child. "What is it, honey?" she asked softly.

"I want you to come back an' live with Daddy an' me!" Nikki wailed. "I couldn't go to sleep last night wiffout your princess story. Daddy tried to tell it, but it wasn't the same. I wanted *you!*"

"She was completely unreasonable," Mrs. Olsen proclaimed.

Sarah clamped her lips together, biting her tongue to keep from telling the old biddy off. She kept her eyes on Nikki. "So what happened, sweetheart?"

"Her father sat up half the night reading her stories, that's what happened," Mrs. Olsen interjected, as if Nikki were incapable of answering. The woman rolled her eyes, indicating that she found Jake's behavior to be completely absurd. "The child finally fell asleep sometime around one in the morning. I told Mr. Masters it would be best to let her cry herself to sleep, but he wouldn't hear of it."

"I should hope not! That's no way to treat—"

The woman raised her chin to a haughty angle and rudely interrupted. "I've been caring for children for thirty years, and believe me, it's best to start off on the right foot. That way everyone adjusts better. You've got to set the rules early and make them stick."

Sarah looked down at the small girl clinging to her leg, thinking of a few things she would like to tell this old goat to go stick. She struggled to keep her voice cool and even. "Rules are important, but not as important as a child's emotional needs."

"Balderdash," sniffed Mrs. Olsen. "That's a bunch of modern-day poppycock."

Outrage, fierce and hot, simmered in Sarah veins. "Why, that's the most…"

"Sarah, dear, the children are ready for their midmorning snack," Deb gently interjected, touching Sarah's arm and motioning her to the other room. Through a haze of indignation, Sarah realized Deb was trying to prevent a confrontation. And she was right, Sarah grudgingly conceded. Nothing she could say was likely to change the nanny's sour attitude. The old bat was so rigid she probably starched her underwear with cement.

Sarah draped her arm around Nikki as Deb skillfully escorted Mrs. Olsen to the door. "I'm afraid you'll have to excuse us, but we have a schedule to keep," Deb told the woman in a pleasant voice. "It was so nice of you to bring Nikki this morning."

Nikki scrunched up her nose and made a face at the housekeeper's retreating back. "I don't like her," she whispered to Sarah.

Sarah didn't, either. The old crone reminded her of the witch in *The Wizard of Oz.*

"Come on, Nikki," Sarah said, forcing a lighter tone into her voice than she felt. "You can help me hand out the juice and crackers. After our snack, it'll be music time. Do you know how to do the hokeypokey?"

The little girl brightened. Sarah only wished that her own thoughts could be so easily diverted.

Sarah sat on the edge of her bed and stared at the phone on her nightstand. Maybe she should call Jake and voice her concerns about Mrs. Olsen.

She'd debated the issue all day. Her head told her it was none of her business: Jake was perfectly capable of working out his household problems for himself.

But a less pragmatic part of her kept reaching for the phone. When Mrs. Olsen had come to pick up Nikki at the end of the day, the child had clung to Sarah and cried, again begging her to come back to the ranch with her.

The episode had wrenched Sarah's heart—especially since there was nothing she would have liked more than to do just that.

Maybe she should call, Sarah thought again, plucking at

a thread on her floral comforter. She lifted the receiver, then dropped it back in its cradle as her eye fell on her alarm clock. Her grandmother had always said it was rude to place calls after nine in the evening, and it was well after eleven. Besides, she didn't want Jake to think she was sitting up pining for him—even if that was exactly what she was doing.

With a sigh, Sarah picked up a novel from her nightstand, but her thoughts wouldn't stay focused on the story. A cold, aching loneliness rested on her heart like a chunk of ice as memories of Jake churned through her: Jake reading to Nikki, his dark head pressed close to his daughter's white-blond curls; Jake standing at the stove, cracking jokes and eggs as he made Sunday breakfast; Jake holding her in front of the mirror, his chest bare, his eyes filled with passion, his hands making her body quiver....

This wasn't helping. Disgusted with her inability to control her thoughts, she flipped off her bedside lamp, hoping to escape into the oblivion of sleep.

She'd no sooner placed her head on the pillow than the doorbell rang. Alarmed, Sarah jumped out of bed, grabbed her robe, and headed for the door. Who on earth would be stopping by at this time of night? Her pulse pounding, she looked through the peephole.

Jake. Her heart rate doubled, and her hand shook so hard that it took her three times longer than normal to unfasten the dead bolt.

He pulled off his black Stetson as she opened the door. "I'm sorry to disturb you this late, Sarah."

"That...that's okay," Sarah managed, clutching her lace-trimmed robe around her, wondering what in the world had brought him here at this hour. "Would you like to come in?"

"I'd better not. Nikki's in the car, and I don't want to leave her alone."

"Is she all right?" Sarah asked worriedly.

"She's fine. Wide-awake, but fine." He shuffled his

stance uneasily and shifted his Stetson to his other hand. "I needed to come talk to you and didn't have anyone to watch her, so I had to bring her with me. Mrs. Olsen resigned and left."

Sarah felt a wave of relief. "Was it her idea or yours?"

"I guess you might say it was mutual." He gave a wry smile. "She thought I should spank Nikki and I told her I'd prefer to spank her instead."

Sarah's eyes grew wide. "You didn't!"

Jake grinned. "'Fraid I did. That dried-up old biddy might have had great references, but her heart's as hard as a prune pit."

Sarah laughed. Jake smiled back. When their eyes met, she suddenly found it hard to breathe.

Jake leaned his hand against the doorjamb. "I hate to ask you this, Sarah, but would you come back and stay at the ranch until I can hire someone else? I've got to go out of town for a few days, and I don't want to leave Nikki with a stranger."

Sarah gazed at him, her heart thudding wildly. Going back to the ranch would be beyond unwise; it would be completely foolhardy. If she missed him this badly now, how much more would it hurt if she got even more deeply attached?

She brushed a strand of hair out of her eyes. "I'd like to help, Jake, but—"

He cut her off before she could finish her thought. "I promise I'll behave myself. I know things got out of hand before, but I won't let it happen again. I respect you too much, Sarah. You deserve..."

He hesitated, and Sarah silently filled in the blanks—*a man who can love you with his whole heart.* Those were the words he'd used the night he'd told her he wanted her, and again the night he'd held her in front of the mirror.

The memories made Sarah ache inside. She briefly closed her eyes, willing herself not to cry.

She opened them to find him looking at her, his brow

furrowed, his eyes dark and filled with—what? Pain? Regret? Sadness? All three, Sarah decided.

"You deserve a whole lot more than I can offer," he finished. He looked away, turning his hat by the brim. "I'll pay you just as before. And if you want to teach while Nikki's at school, that's fine with me." His eyes flicked back to hers, knocking the wind out her. All he had to do was look at her, and she grew weak with wanting him. "Please say you'll come back, Sarah. Nikki and I need you."

Nikki and I need you. The words burrowed under her skin, dived into her bloodstream, and rushed straight to her heart. Couched in those terms, he could have asked for anything or everything, and she gladly would have granted his request.

Had he known that? Was that why he'd said it?

Sarah was beyond caring. Her head was already so far over her heels that she would have welcomed any excuse to be with him and Nikki for a little while longer.

Sarah nodded. "I'll bring Nikki home from school tomorrow and plan to stay."

Jake ran his hand across his jaw. "I know it's late, but could you come now? Nikki won't go to sleep unless you tuck her in with the princess story, and I'm pretty desperate."

A rush of warmth, sweet and rich as hot chocolate, poured through her. What Jake thought was a terrible inconvenience, Sarah saw as a precious gift. How wonderful, how soul-satisfying, to be so urgently needed. All of her life she'd longed to be needed like this.

Sarah knew her smile was ridiculously wide, but she couldn't seem to tone it down. "Give me a moment to grab a few things, and I'll be right with you."

Sarah tossed a dandelion onto the growing pile of weeds beside the garden, then sat back on her heels and wiped the perspiration from her forehead with the back of her cotton gardening glove. It was only ten in the morning, but the late-June sun was already broiling hot.

It had been cooler when she and Nikki had started their Saturday gardening an hour earlier, but the sight of a shirtless Jake, muscles bulging as he rehung the freshly painted shutters on the house windows, had made it feel like high noon. Sarah had tried to stay focused on clearing the rows of vegetables and the adjacent bed of flowers, but her eyes had kept straying to Jake. She'd been relieved when the mother of one of Nikki's friends from preschool had telephoned and invited Nikki over to play. By the time Sarah had returned from giving the child a ride to her friend's home, Jake was working on the front of the house, out of Sarah's line of vision.

Unfortunately, Sarah thought as she tugged another weed from the soil, out of sight didn't mean out of mind. Jake was never far from her thoughts these days. In the past two-and-a-half weeks since she'd returned to the ranch, her feelings for him had grown faster than the dandelions, despite the fact he'd been gone for much of that time.

Maybe it was *because* he'd been gone, Sarah mused. He'd attended a cattlemen's convention, gone to a cattle auction, and made three shorter trips to acquire new breeding stock. Wherever he was and whatever he was doing, though, he called to check on Nikki every evening. And each time he phoned, he wound up in a lengthy conversation with Sarah.

Talking to Jake long-distance was entirely different from talking to Jake in person. On the phone, he was warm, relaxed, amusing—even flirtatious. In person, he was polite but distinctly reserved. He no longer obviously went out of his way to avoid her, but he made a point of never being alone with her.

The result was that she felt closer to him when he was away. He was so determined to avoid involvement that he only let down his guard at a distance, she thought with frustration.

And yet she sometimes caught Jake watching her with a hungry, wistful look on his face that made her heart bounce around in her chest like a tennis ball. She'd noticed him looking at her like that last night in Nikki's room while she was telling the princess story, and she'd grown so flustered she'd accidentally used the mayor's deep baritone voice for one of Princess Rose's lines.

Just her luck, she thought woefully, jabbing at a stubborn weed with her hand spade. She'd finally found a man who thought she was attractive, a man who made her feel special and appreciated and beautiful for the first time in her life, a man who was everything she'd ever dreamed of—and more. But he was so bitterly dead-set against any kind of romantic involvement that he wouldn't even stay alone in the same room with her for more than two minutes.

It was just as she'd feared when she'd agreed to move back in—the more she saw of him, the more she talked with him, the more she watched him with Nikki, the more she cared about him. The more she cared about him, the more she wanted him to love her in return. And the more she wanted what he was determined not to give, the more she hurt.

Sarah plucked another weed from the soil, toying again with the idea of seduction. She'd pondered the concept ever since she'd moved back to the ranch. She had it all planned out; she could wait until Nikki was asleep, then don her sheerest nightgown, tiptoe down the hall, and crawl into bed with him.

Would he throw her out of the bed or make love to her? Sarah shivered at the possibilities. She was just desperate enough to try it. There was only one major flaw in the scheme—it wouldn't solve the real problem. The problem wasn't that Jake was incapable of love, as he claimed; the problem was that he wouldn't allow it. If she got too close or if he started to feel the things she longed for him to feel, he would cut her out of his life. If he ever made love to her, she was certain he would send her packing the very next morning.

Sarah jerked at a clump of Johnsongrass, taking her frustrations out on the unwanted plant. Jake hadn't made any moves to try to hire another housekeeper, but Sarah knew she would have to leave soon anyway. Her heart couldn't take too much more of this. For the sake of her pride and self-esteem, she was going to have to get on with her life.

But not just yet. For just a little while longer, she wanted to stay here and store up memories to warm the long, cold nights for the rest of her lonely life.

Attacking the weeds with a vengeance, Sarah worked her way into the flower bed, weeding a row of tall chrysanthemums near a dense stand of blackberry bushes at the back of the garden. She reached under the blackberry brambles to pull out a clump of crabgrass and felt something slither across her wrist.

Sarah froze, her arm extended. *Oh, dear Lord—a snake.* Her heart filled her throat, choking off her air supply. Paralyzed with horror, she saw the hideous creature wriggle over the bare skin of her arm. It was long and black and terrifyingly lumpy, as if it had eaten something too large to digest. It seemed to move in slow motion as it made its way across her wrist and over her gardening glove to slink into the dark recesses in the bushes.

Sarah didn't know when she started screaming. She only knew that she couldn't stop.

Jake heard a series of high-pitched, bloodcurdling shrieks—so shrill that the hair on the back of his neck stood up. "What in blazes..." he muttered.

The realization hit him like a cement block. *Sarah!*

Adrenaline pumped through his veins, fueled by raw, stark terror. Something unspeakable must have happened to make levelheaded, calm, steady Sarah scream like that. It sounded as if she were being murdered.

Throwing down the heavy black shutter, he climbed

down the ladder and dashed around the house, cursing his injured leg for slowing his speed.

He found her cowering on the ground at the back of the garden, still shrieking. He raced up and knelt beside her, cautiously touching her back, afraid she was injured, not wanting to hurt her further. "What is it? What happened?" he asked urgently.

She turned toward him, her eyes so wild and filled with fear that he wasn't sure she could see him even though she was looking directly at him. A fresh burst of fear tore through him. Firmly grasping her shoulders, he put his face near hers. "Sarah, are you hurt?"

Her screams became hysterical sobs. Still holding her by the shoulders, Jake gave her a gentle shake. "Sarah, honey, calm down and tell me what happened."

Her arms abruptly clutched him, and she buried her face against his chest. Her tears were wet and hot against his naked skin.

"Sn-sn-sn-snake!" she finally managed to gasp between sobs.

"Were you bitten?"

"N-n-n-no!" The word ended in a wail as she sobbed uncontrollably.

Jake didn't know anything about hysteria, but he was pretty sure that was the state she was in. And he didn't think lying here in the dirt was helping matters.

"Everything's okay, Sarah. I'm here, and the snake is gone. But I think you'll be more comfortable in the house." Abruptly he picked her up and carried her across the lawn, one arm under her back, the other under her knees. For a woman of her height, she felt surprisingly light.

He propped her on his good leg as he opened the door, then carried her through the kitchen to the living room. The wooden blinds on the windows were closed, making the room comfortingly cool and dark.

Sarah was still sobbing as Jake gently lowered her to the sofa. She clung to his neck, pulling him down with her.

He sat beside her, awkwardly patting her back, wanting to comfort her but not knowing how. "Can I get you something—a drink? A cool cloth? Tell me how I can help."

"H-h-h-hold m-m-me," she sobbed.

So he did. He hauled her onto his lap, wound one hand around her back, and stroked her hair with his other one, comforting her as he would console Nikki. She sat there and cried, until at long last her racking sobs subsided to a soft mewling sound. A few moments more and they stopped altogether.

Sarah sniffed loudly, drew a deep, wobbly breath and lifted her head from his shoulder. "I'm sorry," she whispered.

Jake ran his hand down her back, his chest tight with emotion. "No need to apologize." He stroked the back of her arm. "Can you tell me what happened?"

"I...I saw a snake." She shivered, and he reflexively tightened his arms around her. "It...it crawled across m-m-my arm and over m-m-my gl-gl-gloves." A fresh sob caught in her throat as she held up her hands.

Jake realized she was still wearing the muddy gloves. He gently took her hands, loosened the fabric on each finger and pulled the gloves off. "What did it look like?" he asked, expertly tossing the gloves into a wicker wastebasket across the room.

"Big and black, and it had a b-b-bulge."

Jake recognized the description. "Sounds like a rat snake. They catch rodents, and they're actually pretty handy to have around."

Sarah closed her eyes and shuddered. She looked like she was about to be ill.

Jake reached up and massaged her neck, trying to figure out what to do next. Lots of people were afraid of snakes, but Sarah's reaction was way beyond the norm. Maybe it would help if she talked about it.

"Why are you so afraid of snakes?"

"I...I had a bad experience once."

"Were you bitten?"

"N-no. I was hu—humiliated."

Jake frowned in confusion. "How could a snake do that?"

Sarah drew a long, raspy breath. "It...it's a long story."

"I've got plenty of time."

She hesitated so long, he didn't think she was going to answer. "It was the summer I turned fifteen," she finally said, shifting so that she was no longer sitting on his lap but beside him. He kept his arm firmly around her, afraid that if he broke contact, she would stop talking and resume crying.

"I was at the height of my gawkiness, and I was in Oak Grove visiting my grandmother for the summer. I developed a terrible crush on a high-school junior named Tommy. I didn't think he knew I was alive. He was really popular, and he hung out with a group of seniors who were all members of a high-school fraternity. And then, out of the blue, he asked me to the Fourth of July dance." Sarah sniffed loudly and drew a deep breath. "I was on cloud nine. I was too flattered and naive to wonder about his motives."

Her voice wavered. A sense of foreboding made Jake tighten his grip on her arm.

"The Fourth of July is a big celebration in Oak Grove. There's a parade, a fair, and a fireworks display. I skipped all the festivities and spent the whole day getting ready for my big date. I was so nervous when Tommy picked me up that I could hardly speak, so I didn't think too much of the fact that he barely said a word to me on the way to the dance. But when we arrived, I thought it was odd that all his friends started laughing. Tommy danced every dance with me, but he kept looking over at his friends, who were snickering on the sidelines."

"What was going on?" Jake asked suspiciously.

Sarah stared down at her fingers in her lap. "I found out when I went to the ladies' room. I heard a girl mention my name just as I walked in, so I stopped in the doorway and listened. She was saying what a shame it was that the high-school fraternity was using me in their hazing ritual. They'd evidently made Tommy bring me to the dance as part of his initiation. The worst part, the girl said, was that I didn't have a clue he was making a fool of me.''

Jake saw red. His chest tightened, and his fingers curled against Sarah's skin. He heard her draw a shaky breath, and knew he needed to let her continue. "She was wrong. The worst part was finding out. I was crushed. I was mortified. I was so humiliated I just wanted to die. If there had been a window in that bathroom, I would have crawled out it. But the only way to get out of the building was to go back through the main hall. I tried to leave, but Tommy pulled me into the middle of the dance floor during a slow dance. I felt so awful, so foolish and conspicuous. And then…''

Sarah's voice broke. She closed her eyes, and all the old, horrible emotions swept over her in a dark, raging tumult, threatening to once more drag her under. Then she felt Jake's arms encircling her, felt his steadying presence beside her. A calm sense of strength flowed through her.

This was all in the past. This could no longer hurt her.

She opened her eyes and met his dark gaze. His eyes were comforting and caring, but the words still stuck in her throat. She swallowed around the large lump that was lodged there and finally blurted it out. "Tommy…Tommy put a snake down the back of my dress. The dress had a tight, fitted waist, and I couldn't get it out. It just slithered around, going from the back to the front, from the front to the back, across my stomach, over my—'' Sarah's voice broke and dissolved.

Jake's arm tautened into a steel band around her. He felt a muscle jerk in his jaw, and his chest tightened in cold fury. "Why, that no-good, rotten son of a—'' He bit off his words in midsentence, knowing anger wouldn't help her, and wanting, above all else, to help her. Her shattered,

woebegone expression made his heart lurch and swell with
tenderness. "Good God, Sarah. How did you handle it?"

"Not well," she admitted shakily. "I became hysterical.
I couldn't even tell anyone what was wrong. I just screamed
and screamed and screamed. Finally, thank heavens, I hy-
perventilated and passed out. Someone called an ambulance. When I came to, I had to be sedated."

Jake swore under his breath. "What happened to that
worthless jerk and his friends?"

Sarah shrugged. "My grandmother saw to it that fraternity initiation practices were discontinued in Oak Grove,
and Tommy's parents grounded him for the rest of the summer."

"He needed to be grounded, all right," Jake muttered
darkly. "Ground into hamburger meat."

A weak smile fluttered across Sarah's lips. "That was
Gran's reaction. I've never seen her so angry. She was such
a sweet, genteel lady, but I think she would have personally
horsewhipped the whole fraternity if she could have."

"What about you? Weren't you angry?"

Sarah sighed and looked away. "I was too destroyed to
feel angry. It was all too late, anyway. Nothing could be
done to take away my sense of humiliation or keep me from
being afraid of snakes or prevent me from dreading the
Fourth of July every year."

Her words wrenched Jake's heart. It was all so senseless,
all so unfair. The thought that Sarah had such deep-seated
scars from a heartless joke pulled by some insensitive
punks made his blood boil. He tried to hide his emotions
with a casual remark. "I take it Independence Day is not
your favorite holiday."

"Oh, I don't get hysterical or anything." Sarah's attempt
to grin was ruined by the wobbling corner of her mouth.
"I just lie low. I haven't been to a Fourth of July celebration since this happened."

Jake's heart twisted again. She looked up at him and
gave another tremulous smile. "You know, I feel a lot bet-

ter since I told you about all this. I haven't talked about it since it happened. I think the fear and shame and all the other stuff I've felt are a lot like the monsters in Nikki's room—they grew in the dark.'' She looked down at her hands, as if she were suddenly embarrassed. ''Thanks for helping me get them out in the open.''

''I'm glad you told me.'' Jake gazed at her, emotion roiling through him, constricting his throat until he could hardly breathe. So many things about her fell into place now—her low self-image, her fear of snakes, her willingness to get involved with that nerd she'd been engaged to. All because of a stupid, cruel high-school prank. A fresh burst of anger pulsed through him, along with an unaccustomed thirst for revenge.

''Is this Tommy character still in town?''

Sarah shook her head. ''He and his family moved the next year. I don't think any of his old friends are still around, either. A lot of the young people in Oak Grove go away to college, then never come back.''

Jake adjusted his arm around her, his heart filled with so much tenderness that his chest ached. He wanted to protect her and hold her and help her heal—to undo all the damage that creep had done to her self-esteem. Feelings for her washed over him, intense and almost overwhelming, making him long to take some action. He was a lot more comfortable with action than emotions. He wished he could figure out a way to help her.

He was suddenly struck by an idea. ''The Fourth is next week. You can spend the day with Nikki and me.''

''Oh, you'll want to take Nikki to the parade and the fair and the fireworks display...''

''And you can come with us.''

Sarah hesitated.

''It'll be good for you, Sarah. You don't want to spend the rest of your life hiding out on the Fourth, do you?''

She looked at him, then slowly shook her head. ''No.''

She drew a deep breath. "Okay. You've got yourself a date."

She smiled up at him, and his breath caught in his throat. She looked so different when she smiled like that. All of a sudden, she felt completely different in his arms, too. He'd been so worried about her, so caught up in comforting her, that he'd blocked out the physical sensation of holding her.

Sensations bombarded him now—rich, sensual impressions that made his blood pump hot and fast: the scent of her hair, the warmth of her skin, the pressure of her breast against his arm. He remembered in vivid, exquisite detail exactly what her breasts had looked like in the lamplight, exactly how they had felt in his hand, exactly how the tips had pebbled against his tongue. His body had an immediate, heated reaction.

His eyes fell to her lips, and the memory of kissing her—how she tasted, how she felt, how she responded—blazed inside him. He ached to kiss her again. He was bending toward her, intent on doing just that, when alarm bells went off in his brain.

It wasn't an actual smoke detector this time, although as hot and bothered as he felt right now, he was in danger of setting one off at any moment. Damn it, he thought, pulling away.

Jake exhaled a harsh blast of air. When he'd begged her to move back to the ranch, he'd promised her this wouldn't happen. He'd promised himself this wouldn't happen. Sarah deserved more than he had to offer, and he wasn't going to lead her on.

Seeing the unmistakable affection radiating from her eyes, he was knifed by a dagger of guilt. Damn it all, she'd been hurt by enough men already. The last thing she needed was to get involved with an overheated cowboy who was sure to cause heartache. He couldn't give her what she really needed, what she wanted deep-down—a husband, a home, a family. He was a bad risk, and she didn't need another bad experience with a man.

He withdrew his arm and rose from the sofa. "Well, if you're okay now, I'd better get back to work." He strode out of the den without waiting for her reply, his emotions churning, his thoughts dark and disjointed, afraid that if he didn't get out of the room, he would break down, break his word and unforgivably break her heart.

Chapter Ten

"**W**ow, this is fun!" Nikki peered over the safety bar as the Ferris-wheel seat swung over the top and started its descent. "I feel like I'm on top of the whole world!"

I feel exactly the same way, but for an entirely different reason. Sarah glanced over Nikki's head and caught Jake's eye. He gave her a slow smile that made her heart spin faster than the Tilt-A-Whirl they'd ridden earlier.

Sarah never would have believed she could enjoy the Fourth of July this much, but the day had been perfect. Jake had made it that way.

He and Nikki and Sarah had gotten up early and headed into town to stake out a prime spot along the parade route—which really hadn't been necessary, Sarah reflected with amusement, since most of the town seemed to be marching in the parade and spectators were in short supply. Nikki had loved the bands and the floats and the beauty queens. Sarah had loved sharing amused looks with Jake as the child jumped up and down, excitedly announcing each new attraction as it rounded the corner.

After the parade, they'd headed to the carnival and craft

show at the county fairgrounds. They'd started out all three holding hands as they'd wended their way through the exhibits, but Nikki kept breaking free and skipping ahead. Before she knew it, Sarah found herself holding hands with just Jake as they followed Nikki through the midway, past the barkers and hawkers and the games, through the rich smells of corn dogs and cotton candy and smoking barbecue, past the competing music from the rides and concessions.

Funny, how something as small as holding Jake's hand could seem so significant. Other people might think they were a couple. Sarah had wondered if Jake realized it and whether he would drop her hand like a hot potato if he did. But when they'd run into Sue Ellen Haskell and stopped to chat, he'd tightened his grip and pulled her closer to his side while the sexy real-estate agent had eyed her venomously.

Worrying she was so unattractive that he would be embarrassed to be seen with her was part of an old, erroneous thought pattern, she mused. It was amazing, how drastically her way of thinking about herself had changed since that night Jake had held her in front of the mirror. The experience had been incredibly freeing. She'd put away her glasses and started wearing her contacts, and she'd bought some flattering new clothes that a salesclerk at the local boutique had helped her pick out. She'd even begun sparingly applying makeup, following a chart in a fashion magazine.

But her biggest change was on the inside. Although she had a lifetime of insecurities to overcome, she no longer felt second-best. Jake had made her feel first-rate—special, wanted, desired. She might not conform to the typical ideal of beauty, but she knew she wasn't a hopeless freak, either. In fact, Jake had shown her that parts of her weren't only attractive but downright sexy.

The way he'd looked at her when he'd seen her this morning in her new red-and-white shorts set had certainly reinforced that, Sarah remembered with a smile. And in case she'd missed the smoldering gleam in his eye, he'd put it into words.

One word, to be exact. "Wow," he'd said, imbuing the expletive with so much masculine appreciation that Sarah's face had grown warm. It grew heated again, just from her thinking about it.

She was startled out of her reverie by something tickling her neck. She turned to Jake, whose arm was stretched across the back of the Ferris-wheel seat, and realized he was twirling a lock of her hair around his finger.

Her stomach did a flip-flop that she couldn't attribute to the ride. He was flirting with her, she thought with something akin to amazement.

She gave him an unsteady grin, unsure how to respond, knowing full well that the reason the day was so wonderful wasn't because of the parade or the fair or even Nikki, whose company always affected Sarah like a ray of sunshine.

It was because Jake was treating her like a date—not like an employee, not like his daughter's preschool teacher, not even like a friend. But like a date—a woman he was attracted to, wanted to know better, and maybe even intended to kiss before the day was over.

A dizzying rush of excitement coursed through her veins as the Ferris wheel again spun through the sky. She gripped the metal bar in front of her, wishing she could get as firm a grip on what Jake was thinking, wishing she knew what he was feeling.

She knew he cared about her. He would never have invited her to join him and Nikki today if he didn't. He'd wanted to help her get over her dread of the holiday, to make sure she didn't spend the day alone with her memories. But how *much* did he care? His flirtatious behavior might be nothing more than a kindly attempt to help her cope on the anniversary of a traumatic event.

And yet, she knew he was attracted to her. She'd felt

unmistakable proof of that the night the smoke detector went off.

The memory made her stomach flutter. Hope, wild and giddy, took flight in her chest. Were his feelings for her strong enough to overcome his bitter heart, to override his determination to never again get involved with a woman?

Her heart pitched like the braking Ferris wheel. She didn't know what tomorrow would bring, but today was too special to ruin with a lot of useless speculation. Just for today, she wanted to live the moment to its fullest, to enjoy it for all it was worth.

"Oh, we're slowing down," Nikki said mournfully.

"It looks like they're going to let the people behind us off first," Jake said. "That means we'll get to go around another time."

"Oh, goody! I wish this ride could last forever."

Me, too, Nikki, Sarah silently concurred, her thoughts far from the Ferris wheel. *Me, too.*

Three hot dogs, two bags of popcorn and one cotton candy later, they wandered through the crafts exhibits.

Sarah stopped at a large booth filled with handmade children's clothing. "Oh, this is beautiful," Sarah said, holding up a plaid jumper appliquéd with apples.

"Thank you," a thin, wiry woman wearing an exhibitor's name tag piped up.

"Did you make this?" Sarah asked, admiring the intricate stitchwork.

The woman nodded proudly.

"It's lovely."

"Yeah, lubbly," Nikki echoed. "I like apples."

"Do you have one in Nikki's size?" Jake asked.

"What size is she?"

Jake rubbed his jaw. "I'm not sure. My former housekeeper always bought Nikki's clothes." He glanced at Sarah, his expression so sheepish her heart turned over.

"I'm, uh, kind of fashion impaired," he confessed. "Especially about girls' stuff."

The woman eyed Nikki appraisingly. "I'd say she's about a 4T." She turned and pulled a jumper off a rack behind her and held it up to the child. "This looks about right."

"Do you like it?" Jake asked Nikki.

The child nodded vigorously. "I wish I could wear dresses every day."

Jake looked at Sarah. "Anything beyond blue jeans, and I'm like a bull in a sheep pen. Would you mind looking around and picking out a few other things for Nikki?"

Mind? It had always been a fantasy of hers to pick out clothing for a little girl. In her dreams, of course, the child had been her own. But Sarah couldn't imagine feeling any more attached to her own child than she did to Nikki. "I'd love to," she said warmly.

"Oh, look!" Nikki exclaimed, jabbing a finger in the air. "A princess gown!"

Sarah looked to where the child was pointing and saw a long pink dress with a filmy overskirt and big, puffy sleeves.

"That's actually a nightgown," the woman said. "It's made completely from fire-retardant materials."

"It's beautiful," Sarah breathed. She glanced quickly at Jake, remembering too late that she probably should have looked to him for a cue before so quickly agreeing with Nikki.

But Jake just smiled. "We'd better get one of those, too." He lowered himself into a chair set against the partition. "And I might as well get comfortable, because I have a feeling we're going to be here for a while."

It feels like we're a family, Sarah mused, smiling to herself as she riffled through the racks of clothes with Nikki. Somewhere in the back of her mind, she knew the thought was inappropriate—knew that it should alarm her that she was getting so close to both Jake and his child. After all, it had nearly killed her to leave before. She was only at their house on a temporary basis, and she would be wise to guard her heart.

But it felt so wonderful to indulge the fantasy. Besides, Jake had made no attempt to find a permanent housekeeper, and he was treating her like a date today. Her pulse accelerated and her hopes soared. Maybe, just maybe...

"Hello there!"

Sarah turned just as Buddy and Hank strolled up, accompanied by their wives. After introductions and small talk, the ranch hands started to move on to the next exhibit. Buddy abruptly stopped short and turned to Jake. "I nearly forgot. You asked a while back if I knew anyone who was good with children, Jake, and it so happens I do. My aunt loves kids, and kids love her. She's a great cook and she runs a mean household. She's a widow. The last of her own kids just left home, and she's looking for a situation just like you described. I'll give you her name and phone number, if you like."

"Thanks, Buddy," Jake said.

Sarah's heart plummeted as the ranch hand scribbled down the information and gave it to Jake. She moved back to the dresses, trying to hide the panic clutching at her chest.

Just because Jake was getting the woman's name didn't mean he was going to send her packing, Sarah rationalized. Buddy hadn't indicated his aunt was in a hurry to find a position.

But if a permanent housekeeper was available, there was no reason for her to stay.

And she desperately wanted to stay. Not as a housekeeper, but as Jake's wife, as Nikki's mother.

Suddenly dizzy, Sarah grasped the end of the dress rack to steady herself. Oh, dear. When had she gotten in so far over her head? Just the thought of leaving made her feel physically ill.

She had the heart of a fool, she thought morosely. Her

head knew that Jake's own heart was bitter and scarred, that he had a mile-high razor-wire fence around it, that the chances of escaping from Alcatraz were better than her chances of breaking through Jake's defenses. But her foolish, dreamy heart had gone ahead and fallen in love with him anyway.

Was there a chance that he might love her back? Her pulse skipped and raced. Two weeks ago, she would have believed it was impossible. But the way Jake was acting today…

"Miz Sarah, do you think Daddy'll let me have some more cotton candy when we finish here?" Nikki asked. "He usually won't let me eat sweets, but it was so good, and the Fourf is a such special day."

Sarah turned and glanced at Jake, who had once again settled in the chair by the wall. He met her gaze with a slow, sexy smile that made her knees turn to Silly Putty. She couldn't help it; her heart inflated with hope, expanding and rising like a birthday-party balloon, defying the odds like helium defied gravity.

"It is a special day," she agreed. "We'll have to see, but on a day as special as this one, anything's possible."

She sent a silent, fervent plea flying heavenward, praying that maybe, just maybe, it might be so.

The sky was a deep twilight purple as Jake and Sarah gathered up the remnants of their barbecued chicken dinner and tucked the picnic supplies into Sarah's large wicker basket.

"This was a great idea, bringing food from the fair out here," Jake remarked, stretching out his legs and leaning back on his elbows. His eyes roamed over the darkened lake as an evening breeze rustled the leaves of the oaks overhead and made the water splash against the shore. A pair of nearby frogs began a deep-throated serenade. He sighed contentedly. "I was ready for a little peace and quiet."

"So was someone else, apparently." Sarah cast a wry smile at Nikki, who was sound asleep at the far end of the large picnic blanket.

Jake followed Sarah's gaze and grinned. Turning back, he watched her close the lid on her basket. "You really came prepared—paper plates, plastic forks, wet wipes, the whole shebang."

Sarah tucked a strand of hair behind her ear. It was a small gesture, one she made often, but it suddenly struck Jake as disturbingly sensuous. "Before I stopped celebrating the Fourth, Gran and I used to picnic here every year while we waited for the fireworks to begin. I brought Gran's basket along in case we wanted to do the same thing."

"I'm glad you did. This is a beautiful spot."

"Years ago, it was my grandfather's favorite fishing hole."

"Will we be able to see the fireworks from here?"

Sarah nodded. "They're launched from a boat in the center of the lake. We'll have as good a view as the crowd on the other shore." She wrapped her arms around her knees and gave a contented sigh. "I had a wonderful time today, but it sure feels good to get away from the crowd."

"I'll second that." Getting Sarah away from the crowd had been on his mind for most of the day. More specifically, he'd been preoccupied with the thought of getting her alone—and with all of the delicious things he would like do to her if he did.

Jake gazed out at the lake, at the distant spot where the dark water seemed to blend into the sky, keenly aware of her beside him, her very nearness a source of arousal. She'd had him in a maddening state of arousal all day long. He'd started out with the high-minded motive of trying to help her through a day fraught with ugly memories. He'd figured it wouldn't hurt to let her know how attractive he found her, since that jerk had made her feel like a sideshow exhibit on this date all those years ago, so he'd decided to flirt with her a little.

A little? a small voice inside asked derisively. Jake shifted his weight uncomfortably, knowing he'd spent the entire day mooning over her like a lovesick coyote. He didn't know when it had happened, but somewhere along the line he'd lost his noble purpose and begun to simply act the way he'd wanted to act around her from the very beginning—like a man pursuing a woman.

He glanced over at her, then quickly looked away. Well, heck, he thought, running a hand through his hair; no one could blame him. She looked hotter than a cayenne pepper in those racy red shorts.

It was hard to believe she'd ever been ridiculed over her appearance. Or that any red-blooded male had ever had any reaction to her besides blood-pounding, toe-tingling, sock-popping attraction.

He gazed at her profile, wondering what she'd looked like as teenager. The thought of her as she must have been at fifteen—gawky and awkward and painfully self-conscious—created a pang in his chest.

It was so unfair, the way the world judged people on the basis of appearance, he mused—and of all the unfair places in the world, high school was the worst. His own experience had been the opposite of Sarah's, but it, too, had been unpleasant. Girls had fawned over him for no reason other than how he looked, with no regard for who he was or what he was like. He'd been nothing more than a status symbol, a trophy to validate the power of their own attractiveness.

But he'd been just as superficial, he reminded himself with chagrin. He'd fallen for Clarissa because she'd seemed like such a challenge, so detached and distant and icily gorgeous. He'd discovered the hard way that a beautiful exterior with no inner substance soon lost all its charm.

He'd ceased thinking of Clarissa as beautiful once he'd really gotten to know her. With Sarah, though, the reverse was happening. The closer he got to her, the more beautiful she became.

He abruptly sat up, uneasy with the direction of his thoughts, not wanting to admit that his feelings for her were so emotionally grounded. There had to be a more rational explanation for her increasing appeal.

Some women just took a while to grow into their looks, and Sarah had grown into hers this summer, that was all.

Boy, had she ever, he mentally added, casting another admiring glance at her. It seemed as if she'd blossomed right before his eyes. He'd been attracted to her the first time he'd seen her, but now he found her virtually irresistible.

His eyes roamed up her tanned legs to the generous swell of her breasts. By the time he looked up at her face, she'd caught him watching her.

She gave a languid smile that made his heart thunder like a cattle stampede. "I really did have a great time today," she said softly, reaching out her hand.

He took her fingers in his. Her hand felt soft and fineboned and exquisitely feminine. "Me, too."

They gazed at each other, attraction crackling between them—the kind of hot, needy attraction that begged to be acted upon.

Easy, boy. Jake drew a deep breath and turned his attention back to the lake, but holding Sarah's hand was like holding the key to paradise. He couldn't help but think of all the places he would like to feel her fingers, all the ways and places he would like to touch her in return.

He realized, though, that once he started, he wouldn't want to stop. She tightened her fingers, and their soft pressure fired a hard, hot surge of desire.

"Do you think the fireworks will start soon?" she asked.

At any moment. He stared at her and swallowed hard. He'd wanted to kiss her all day, and he didn't know how much longer he could hold out. He was fast losing touch with all the reasons why he should.

He made a guttural sound of assent. Sarah turned her gaze back to the water. It was deep dusk, almost dark, but he could still make out the details of her profile—the wispy outline of her bangs, the sweep of her lashes, the delicate curve of her cheekbone. Before he realized what he was doing, he'd reached out and touched her face.

She turned toward him, her eyes talking, their gray depths singing a siren's song. Her lips softened and parted. When she spoke, her voice was low and husky and deadly serious. "If you don't kiss me soon, Jake, I think I'll die."

His control snapped like a brittle twig. He hauled her into his arms and claimed her mouth, all caution abandoned, all rational thought forgotten, everything overridden by hot, hungry need.

Her lips were all he remembered and more—soft and slick and demanding. Her mouth opened under his, and she pressed herself against him, flattening her breasts on his chest, pushing him back on the blanket.

The full length of Sarah stretched out on top of him made his blood boil. She was warm and soft and eager. Holding nothing back, she made no pretense of being composed or sophisticated or smooth. She was all knees and elbows and hot, wanting woman, and he felt like his heart would burst with the fullness of all he felt for her.

He opened his eyes and gazed into her face just as a skyrocket burst overhead; and the truth burst upon him as well, exploding in a brilliant, blinding stream of light. She'd gotten to him. He was crazy about her—besotted, obsessed, completely smitten. When he was around her, he was as out of control as a bull full of locoweed.

The air in his lungs compressed, making his chest hot and heavy. He had the horrible, sinking feeling of a man who didn't know how to swim but who'd just discovered he was in water way over his head.

A wave of panic swept over him. Dear God, he hadn't meant for things to get this far out of hand.

He looked into her eyes and saw a mirror image of what

he felt for her beaming back at him. His stomach twisted and knotted. Damn it, he hadn't meant to lead her on. The last thing on earth he wanted was to hurt her. He didn't have a road map for "happily ever after," and that was what she needed, what she deserved.

"Sarah, honey…" He struggled to sit up. Sarah sat up with him, clinging to his neck.

"Don't," she whispered. Her hands moved to his face. She placed a soft finger over his lips. "Don't think. Don't talk. Just feel."

She drew his face down and kissed him, her mouth so urgent and sweet and hot that it burned every thought from his mind. He was in the grip of something stronger than all of his convictions, stronger than his will to fight it. With a groan, he pulled her to him and deepened the kiss.

"Is Miz Sarah gonna be my new mommy?"

Jake froze, then jerked away as if he'd been doused with gasoline and Sarah held a lit match. He whipped around to see Nikki sitting cross-legged on the far edge of the blanket, watching them with avid curiosity.

"Uh, hi, honey." Jake nervously cleared his throat. "Miss Sarah and I were just…"

"You were kissin'. I saw." The child grinned so broadly her smile nearly slid off her face. She bounced up and down, vibrating with excitement. A brilliant explosion of green lit the sky, but Nikki ignored the fireworks. "So are you and Miz Sarah gonna get married?"

Oh, Jeez, now he'd gone and done it. Jake cleared his throat again, deliberately avoiding Sarah's eyes. "No, honey, we're not."

Nikki's face fell. "But you were kissin'. I saw."

"Just because two people kiss doesn't mean they're going to get married, honey."

Nikki's brow scrunched up like a troll doll's. "Why not?"

"Well, sometimes it just means they like each other a lot."

"But couldn't you get married? Miz Sarah would make the best mommy in the whole wide world."

The child's words chipped away at Sarah's heart. She peered over at Jake, but he was avoiding her gaze.

"I'm not ever going to marry anybody, honey," Jake said gently.

"But I want a mommy, an' Miz Sarah is jus' perfeck."

Oh, she should have seen this coming, Sarah castigated herself. She loved Nikki so much she'd been fantasizing that she was her daughter. It was only natural that Nikki would start wishing for the same thing, too.

"You and I are doing fine together, just the two of us." Jake's voice was tight and terse.

"But it's more better wif Miz Sarah. Ever'thin's more better wif her."

Another piece of Sarah's heart cracked and broke off.

Jake drew a deep breath and ran a hand down his face, then gave a brittle smile. "Come on, let's watch the fireworks, and then we'll all get some ice cream before we head home."

A huge chrysanthemum-shaped explosion lit the sky, blazing brilliantly for a few scant seconds, then fizzling and falling. The sparks burned out before they hit the water.

Her chest hollow, her throat tight, Sarah watched the last of the embers fade into the dark. Just like her hopes, she thought bitterly. Just like her future with Jake. Just like the pieces of her heart.

Chapter Eleven

"I'd prefer that you live here during the week. I'm up before dawn seeing to the ranch, so I need someone to fix Nikki's breakfast, get her dressed, and take her to school in the mornings. You'd have your own room and bath. On weekends, of course, you'd be free to do as you pleased."

Sarah froze in the hallway, just outside the kitchen door. She could see Jake, his back toward her, the telephone to his ear, his thick mahogany hair gleaming in the first rays of morning light streaming through the kitchen windows. She didn't mean to eavesdrop on his conversation, but her hammering heart seemed to have nailed her feet to the floor.

He shifted his weight and switched the phone to his other ear. "When can you start? Would Monday be too soon?" A brief silence followed. "Good. I'm looking forward to having you join our household, Mrs. Worth. Buddy spoke very highly of you, and I put a lot of stock in Buddy's judgment. I'll see you first thing Monday morning."

The phone thudded back into its cradle. Too dazed and heartsick to move, Sarah was still standing in the doorway when Jake turned around.

"Sarah." Guilt shadowed his face. "I, uh, didn't know you were there."

Numbly, she nodded, forcing herself to walk into the room.

Jake rammed a hand through his hair. "Listen, we, uh— We need to talk. In view of everything, I think it's best if..."

Sarah closed her eyes, bracing herself. She'd known this was coming. Ever since Nikki had caught them kissing last night, she'd known Jake was going to cut her out of his life. All the same, she couldn't bear to hear him say it. She held up her hands. "I understand." She drew a deep breath and tried to keep her voice from quavering. "I...I'll go pack my things."

"Sarah... Wait."

Hesitating at the door, she turned toward him. His brow was lined, and his eyes looked pained. "There's no hurry. It's Saturday. Come sit down, and I'll fix you breakfast. You don't have to go right now."

"Oh, yes, I do." *Before I start thinking about all the dreams I wove around you and all the feelings you awakened in me. Before I'm reminded of how you helped me see myself through a new pair of glasses. Before I burst into tears and lose whatever tiny shred of dignity I still possess.*

Pain slashed through her like a jagged piece of glass. She'd known the pain, too, was coming; it was the penalty for having such a foolish heart, for pretending that the inevitable wasn't just that.

Tears stinging her eyes, Sarah turned and fled to her bedroom.

I won't cry. I won't, she told herself fiercely, jerking open a drawer. She hauled out her lingerie and stacked it on the bed, then yanked open the next and took out her neatly folded jeans. She would collect her things as quickly as possible and try to get away before Nikki woke up. She would get in her car. She would drive back to her lonely house. She would close the door and lock it behind her.

Then, only then, would she allow herself to give way to the torrent of tears building inside her.

"Sarah." Jake stood in the doorway of her room, his eyes bleak and dark, his voice entreating. "Jeezum Pete, I hate for things to end this way. I don't want you to go away all upset. I never—" He blew out a harsh breath of air and thrust a hand into his pocket. "I never meant to hurt you."

She grabbed her large brown suitcase from the closet, plopped it on the bed and yanked it open. In herky-jerky movements, she began piling it with clothes, deliberately keeping her face turned away. "What makes you think you have?"

"By the way I'm hurting."

Her heart thudded heavily in her chest, full of all the things she wanted to say. *Why do you have to be so mule-headed about not getting involved? You're not your father; I'm not your late wife. We're good for each other: we're good for Nikki. Why can't you let go of the past and have a little faith in the future, a little faith in yourself?*

She stared at him, dying inside, and the words all died on her tongue. What good would it do to say any of that to a man who didn't want her love, who refused to love her in return?

He'd said she deserved a man who could love her with his whole heart. How ironic, Sarah thought bitterly, slamming the suitcase lid and clicking the metal fasteners into place. Thanks to the newfound sense of self-esteem he'd helped her discover, she knew he was right. But she also recognized she needed to love that way in return. One of the saddest things about this entire miserable situation was that in her heart of hearts, she knew she would never love another man as wholeheartedly as she loved Jake Masters.

"Miz Sarah, why're you packin' up your stuff?"

Sarah looked up to see Nikki standing next to Jake in the doorway, wearing her new princess nightgown and clutching her ragged teddy bear. The child stared at her, round-eyed and worried.

Panic raced through Sarah. Her gaze flicked to Jake, who looked as discomfited as she felt. "It...it's time for me to move back to my own house, honey. Your daddy's found a permanent housekeeper."

Nikki's lower lip wobbled precariously. "I don't want a perm'nen' keeper. I want you!"

"I'll still see you every day at school, sweetheart."

"But you won' be *here*."

"No, but you'll have me and Mrs. Worth," Jake interjected. "She's a very nice lady. She's Buddy's aunt, and I'm sure you'll grow to love her."

"Not like I love Miz Sarah." The child ran across the room and threw her arms around Sarah. "I'll never love anyone like I love Miz Sarah. I want her to stay an' be my mommy."

Sarah saw the child's tear-spattered face and felt her heart break anew. Tears in her own eyes, Sarah gazed pleadingly at Jake.

"Come on, Nikki, I'll fix you breakfast. Let's let Miss Sarah pack in peace," he urged.

"Nooooo!" The high-pitched wail grew muffled when the child buried her wet face against Sarah's chambray skirt. "I don' want her to go-o-o!"

Sarah stroked Nikki's soft hair, tears choking her throat, helpless to speak.

"Nikki, we've got to let Miss Sarah pack. Are you going to come with me, or do I have to carry you out of here?"

The child only wailed louder and clung more tightly to Sarah. His eyes full of pain, Jake finally strode across the room, picked his daughter up and carried her, bawling like a calf in a hailstorm, out of the room.

I won't cry. I won't. She couldn't give in to her emotions now, Sarah told herself fiercely, drawing a deep breath and fighting back the maelstrom of tears damming behind her eyes; she needed to figure out a way to make this easier on

Nikki. If the child was taking it this hard now, bedtime would be a nightmare.

Inspiration, the kind born of despair and desperation, suddenly struck. *A tape.* She could make a tape of the princess story and leave it on Nikki's bed. The child now had a recorder and some blank tapes in her room.

On trembling legs, Sarah headed for the hallway, pausing at the door long enough to determine that Jake and Nikki were downstairs. She would record the princess story while she finished packing. Hopefully the tape would ease the separation for Nikki. And maybe, just maybe, making it would keep Sarah from falling apart long enough to collect her things and get out of the house.

The bell jangled overhead as Jake opened the door to Happy Times Preschool on Wednesday morning, echoing the condition of his nerves. Mrs. Worth had been bringing Nikki to school for the past two days, and Jake hadn't seen Sarah since she'd fled the ranch on Saturday—hadn't seen her in the flesh, that was. He'd seen her a million times in his mind's eye—every time he walked through the kitchen, each time he passed the garden, at night when he lay restlessly thrashing in bed in a room wallpapered in a pattern Sarah had selected, in the fractured dreams that haunted him when he finally succumbed to exhausted sleep.

He spotted her immediately, his eye drawn to her like a hummingbird to a brilliant blossom. She sat on the floor, surrounded by a semicircle of preschoolers, reading from an oversize book. She was wearing a bright pink shorts outfit that showed off her figure and made her complexion glow. He hesitated in the doorway, his heart lurching in his chest.

She glanced up, saw him and froze in midsentence.

Deb rushed forward from somewhere at the back of the room. "I'll take it from here, Sarah," she said, taking the book and easing her girth onto the floor with the children.

Sarah slowly rose and walked to the entrance, her expression guarded. "Where's Nikki? Is she sick today?"

"No." Jake thrust his hands into his pockets, feeling uncomfortable. "Can we step outside?"

He held the door open, and Sarah stepped through. The July heat rose up and met them, enveloping them like a blanket. They stood in the narrow ledge of shade provided by the building's porch. *Might as well get it over with,* Jake thought grimly. "I, uh, came by to tell you that I'm taking Nikki out of your school."

Sarah's lips parted and her eyes clouded with pain. Jake winced. Damn it, he hated himself right now, but he was doing what he had to do. It was for Sarah's sake as well as Nikki's, he reminded himself.

He looked down at the toe of his brown boot, trying to steel himself, then gazed back up at her face. "I figured I owed it to you to tell you in person. It has nothing to do with the school. You're a terrific teacher, and I love everything she's been learning here. But it's just too hard on her, seeing you every day. Mrs. Worth's told me about the crying jags she goes through every time she picks her up at the end of the day." Jake ran a hand down his face. "And she's crying a lot at home, too. I just think it would be easier on her—on everybody—if we make a clean break of it."

Sarah's body was so stiff she looked like a calf frozen in a snowstorm. "I...I see."

"I've enrolled her at The Learning Tree," he said, naming the town's other preschool.

Sarah inhaled sharply. He saw her swallow. "It's...it's a good school."

Criminy, she was too nice to be believed. It made him hate himself all the more for hurting her. "I just don't want to see Nikki so unhappy," he explained. "And I don't imagine this has been very easy on you, either."

"So your solution is to separate us because she cares about me, is that it?" Sarah's voice was suddenly hot and tight. "Tell me, Jake, do you intend to do this every time she gets too close to a woman?"

For the first time since he'd known her, her eyes spat fire. Her anger caught him off guard, like an unexpected punch in the gut. "No, of course not."

"Oh, I see. It's just me." Sarah placed her hands on her hips and regarded him heatedly. "What exactly have I done that's so awful?"

"You haven't done anything wrong. You know that." He raked a hand through his hair and shifted his stance, hating the conversation...the situation...himself. "You've been wonderful. Too wonderful, if you want to know the truth. In fact, you've been so dadblasted, all-fired wonderful that Nikki's fixated on the idea of you becoming her mother. And I don't want to encourage her to yearn and dream for something that's never going to happen."

And you *shouldn't, either.* The words hovered between them, unspoken but not unheard. Sarah's eyes darkened with pain, and her lips trembled before she resolutely clamped them together.

"I'll go gather up Nikki's things," she mumbled, turning and slipping through the door, but not before he saw the shimmer of a tear on her cheek.

Jake stared out at the street, cursing himself for hurting her. He'd been wrong to ever let things get so far out of hand.

He was out his depth, beyond the realm of his experience. All he knew about relationships was that they hurt like hell when they ended, and he didn't want to ever gamble on one again. The stakes were too high, and too many people would be affected. Look how everyone was hurting now, he thought bitterly.

Sarah returned a few minutes later, the contents of Nikki's cubby in a plastic bag.

Jake took the bag from her. Awkwardness stretched between them. "Listen, Sarah... You saved our lives when I was down for the count." Setting the bag on the ground, he pulled out his wallet and dug out several hundred-dollar bills. "I know I'll never be able to repay you, but I'd like you to accept this as a token of my appreciation."

Sarah stared at the money in his outstretched hand. "I don't want your money."

"Take it," he urged. "It'll make me feel better."

Sarah's eyes glittered with outrage and hurt. "You just don't get it, do you? Well, let me clue you in. Love is a gift. You can't buy it, you can't pay it off, and you can't control it. You can't shrink it down to a manageable size, or box it in, or dole it out in amounts you're comfortable with. It just *is*."

Her eyes blazed like blue-gray flames. "You think you don't have enough to go around. And you know what? As long as you think that, you'll be right. You *won't* have enough. Because love is a funny thing, Jake. In order to have it, you've got to give it away."

She turned on her heel and walked through the door, letting it slam behind her. It sounded eerily like the door of a prison cell, locking him out, locking him up, locking away something he hadn't known he needed until it had already been yanked away.

"Sarah, this is Mary over at The Learning Tree."

Sarah's pulse jumped and raced, her thoughts immediately flying to Jake and Nikki. She nervously shifted the phone to her other ear, trying to keep an eye on a pair of preschoolers in the art center who were up to their elbows in finger paint. "Hi, Mary. What's up?"

"Is Nikki Masters with you, by any chance?"

The worry in the woman's voice sent a jolt of alarm surging through Sarah's veins. "No. I haven't seen her since last week...not since she transferred to your school. Why do you ask?"

"Because she's gone."

Sarah's heart stopped. When it resumed beating, it

drummed at twice its normal speed. "What do you mean, gone?"

"Well, she was here an hour ago." Mary's voice sounded thin and anxious through the receiver. "She must have sneaked inside and gone out the front door while we were all playing on the playground equipment in the backyard. I was hoping that maybe you'd come and picked her up. She kept talking about you, and earlier in the day she said she was going to see you. Her bag with her favorite bear and blanket is gone, so I thought maybe..." Mary's voice trailed off and disappeared like a vapor trail. "Oh, dear. Well, I'd better call the police. Her father will be here to pick her up at any moment. Sorry to have bothered you."

Sarah hung up the phone, dazed and scared, her heart pounding wildly. Nikki had been preying on her thoughts continually ever since Jake had removed her from the school. She wasn't just fond of the child; she loved her. Just as she loved Jake.

Deb looked at her sharply. "You look a little green around the gills. What's wrong?"

"Nikki's missing. And I have a horrible feeling she's run away to come find me." Sarah quickly filled her in, clutching the back of a child-size red chair to support her suddenly feeble knees. "It's all my fault, Deb. I've got to go help find her."

Deb's face creased in a worried frown. "This isn't your fault at all, but go on ahead. I'll hold down the fort here until all our students are picked up by their parents, then I'll come help."

"Thanks, Deb," Sarah muttered gratefully, grabbing her purse and heading to her car. *Dear God,* she prayed, sliding behind the wheel, *please be with Nikki. Please keep her safe from harm, and please, please let us find her soon.*

The Learning Tree was on the opposite side of town, and by the time Sarah pulled up in front of the school, Oak Grove's two police cars were already there. So was Jake's truck, Sarah noted, slamming her car door and racing to the school entrance.

She found Mary, the small, dark-haired proprietor of the school, seated in her tiny office, hanging up the phone. Her usually ruddy face was ashen.

"Any word?" Sarah asked anxiously.

She shook her head. "The police are combing the area. They've already searched the blocks immediately around the school and found nothing."

"Where's Nikki's father?"

"Out with the police."

"I'll go out, too." Sarah turned to leave, but the haunted look in Mary's eyes tugged at her heart. She hesitated, her hand on the door. "It'll be all right, Mary."

"I sure hope so. It'll be dark in a few hours."

"She couldn't have gone far," Sarah said softly.

"If...if nobody picked her up." A sob tore from Mary's throat. "Oh, Sarah, I feel so responsible! If anything happens to that child..." Crying, Mary buried her face in her hands.

A cold chill skidded up Sarah's spine. Memories of every horrible news story she'd ever read about a missing child floated through her mind, each more terrifying than the one before. Fighting a rising tide of panic, she gave Mary a consoling hug. "We'll find her," she said with more confidence than she felt.

The woman nodded and drew a halting breath, obviously trying to pull herself together. Sarah gave her a final squeeze, then headed out the door.

But she had no idea how to proceed. Sarah hesitated in the drive, stuffing her hands in the pockets of her khaki walking shorts. Should she drive around and look for the child, or search for her on foot? What could she possibly do that the police weren't already doing? She didn't know; she only knew she couldn't sit around and idly wait.

Whatever she was going to do, she needed to do it fast. The late-afternoon sun was riding low in the sky.

She would try to put herself in Nikki's shoes and think like a four-year-old, Sarah decided. Nikki had evidently come out the front door. The natural way for her to go would be straight ahead.

Following her instincts, Sarah roamed the neighborhood sidewalks, calling the child's name, periodically crossing paths with a police officer or the slow-cruising sheriff's vehicle. Half an hour later, despair settled over her like fog on the lake. Her efforts were useless, she thought. The entire neighborhood had evidently already been thoroughly canvased. Disheartened, she was about to turn back, when all of a sudden she stopped in her tracks.

Was it her imagination, or had she heard something? "Nikki!" she called again.

"Miz Sarah?"

Sarah's heart thudded deliriously. "Yes, honey, it's me. Where are you?"

The branches parted on an enormous azalea bush in front of the house across the street, and the child stepped onto the lawn.

Sarah ran toward her. "Nikki!" Kneeling on the grass, she caught the girl in an enormous bear hug.

The passing police car screeched to a halt, and the next thing Sarah knew, Jake was beside her, embracing his daughter. Nikki threw an arm around each of their necks, then the three of them were hugging each other as tears of joy streamed down Sarah's face. She gazed at Jake, her heart thundering madly, and for a split second, the world was brilliant, beautiful, blindingly bright.

"Sweetheart, where were you? What happened?" Jake finally asked.

"I was tryin' to find Miz Sarah, an' I got lost."

"We've been looking and looking for you! Didn't you hear us calling you? Where have you been?"

"I heard some men callin', an' I got scared 'cause I know I'm not s'posed to talk to strangers, so I hid." Nikki gave Sarah a toothy, beaming grin. "But I rec'nized Miz Sarah's voice, so I came out."

"Thank heavens." Jake's eyes rested on Sarah, warming her like an electric blanket.

"Excuse me, Mr. Masters," interrupted a deep voice. Sarah turned to see a tall, potbellied police officer standing behind them, a clipboard in his hand. "I know you're anxious to take your little girl home, so why don't we go back to the school and finish up the paperwork so you can be on your way."

"Fine." Jake straightened, then reached out his arms to pick up Nikki.

"I want Miz Sarah to carry me," the child proclaimed.

Sarah gazed hesitantly at Jake. Her arms ached to hold the child, but she wasn't sure of his reaction. She was all too aware that the reason he had changed schools in the first place was because of her growing closeness to Nikki.

But Jake just nodded. "Okay by me."

Nikki hurled herself at her. Her heart as full as her arms, Sarah carried the child to the waiting police car. The three of them rode back to The Learning Tree, where Mary and Deb greeted them with shouts of joy.

Twenty minutes later, the policeman flipped his notebook closed. "Well, that does it. I'm glad we found your daughter, Mr. Masters." The officer squatted down beside Nikki, who was sitting at a low table with Deb and Mary, working on a puzzle. "And no more running away, young lady. Will you promise me that?"

"I promise," Nikki said. "'Sides, since Miz Sarah's here, I don' need to go lookin' for her."

Jake and Sarah exchanged an uneasy glance. Jake rose from his chair. "Well, it's time to go home, sport."

"Is Miz Sarah gonna come, too?" Nikki asked eagerly.

Jake turned to her. "I wish you would, Sarah." His eyes were dark and serious, and something about them made her stomach flutter wildly.

Deb looked at them, then glanced meaningfully at Mary.

"Come on, Nikki. Why don't you and I and Miss Mary give your dad and Miss Sarah a moment of privacy."

"What's privacy?"

"I'll explain it on the way outside."

The door banged shut as they filed out. The room suddenly seemed too quiet, too intimate. Jake's Adam's apple bobbed as he swallowed. "I'd like for you to come back to the ranch for dinner. We need to talk, Sarah. "

Sarah ran a trembling hand through her hair. "There's nothing to talk about. Besides, I don't want to give Nikki reason to hope for things that will never be."

And I don't want to hope for the impossible, either, she told herself. *It's too difficult seeing you, seeing Nikki, loving you both, knowing I'll never be a part of your lives.*

Jake studied her, his brown eyes troubled. "Well, maybe we can work something out."

Sarah curled her fingers so tightly that her fingernails bit into the palm of her hand, hoping the pain would keep her focus off the greater pain threatening to shatter in her chest. "I don't think so, Jake. The differences between us aren't going to disappear with a conversation."

They gazed at each other, tension stretching between them like a taut, vibrating wire. His eyes churned with turmoil and emotion.

She thought for certain he was going to touch her. If he did, she would melt. She would go with him then and there; she would agree to anything or everything. She was aching for his touch, dying for it.

But their eyes remained the only point of contact.

"I'd better go," he finally said, his voice low and rocky.

Sarah nodded and turned away, not wanting him to see the tears in her eyes. She heard the door close behind him, heard Deb and Mary call their goodbyes, heard Jake's truck roar to life, then heard the tires crunch on the graveled driveway.

Hot tears spilled down her cheeks. She furiously wiped

them away with the back of her hand as the door squeaked open again, and Deb and Mary stepped into the room.

"I'd better be going, too," Sarah mumbled. "I'm glad it all worked out."

Deb followed her out the door, her eyes concerned. "Sarah, honey, why on earth didn't you go with Jake? This episode really shook him up. Nikki told me that she wanted you to be her mother, but her father doesn't want to get married again. Now that he realizes how much Nikki loves you and needs you, he might change his mind about marriage."

Sarah stared down at her tennis shoes. "That isn't good enough, Deb."

"What on earth do you mean?"

She looked into her friend's warm, caring eyes. "I don't want a marriage based on need or convenience. I want a marriage like you and Harry have—one that's based on genuine love. Jake told me I shouldn't settle for less than a man who can give his whole heart, and he's right. That's what I've got to offer. And that's what I want in return." The lump in her throat made it hard to continue. She swallowed hard. "But I don't know if Jake will ever be able to give anyone his whole heart. I'm not even sure he has all of it left to give. Sometimes I think it's been eaten away by bitterness." A tear streaked down her cheek, and she impatiently wiped it away.

Deb's brow wrinkled with concern. She opened her arms and enfolded Sarah in a motherly hug. "Why don't you come home with me? I don't think you should be alone tonight."

"I've got to get used to it sometime, and there's no time like the present."

Giving Deb a final squeeze, Sarah walked to her car, closed the door, and drove off into the twilight. The future seemed as drab and forlorn as the falling dusk—a future without Jake, without Nikki, without the center of her heart.

* * *

Jake's fingers tightened on Wildfire's reins later that night as he stared out at the pasture, then up at the star-filled sky. The stallion shifted restlessly beneath him—but not as restlessly as Jake's thoughts shifted through his mind.

He'd saddled up the roan and mounted him this evening for the first time since his accident. Riding had always been a source of solace to Jake, and tonight he'd needed an outlet for his frazzled nerves. His emotions had been in turmoil ever since he'd learned of Nikki's disappearance.

The thought of Nikki made him sigh. She was asleep now, under the watchful eye of Mrs. Worth, but it had taken nearly two hours to get her that way. Putting Nikki to bed had become a nightly ordeal. Mrs. Worth and Jake took turns rocking the child, reading to her, even singing to her, but all Nikki wanted to do was listen to Sarah's tape and cry.

The grandmotherly older woman had stopped him in the hall earlier in the evening. "If you don't mind my saying so, Mr. Masters, I think you ought to try to get Sarah back permanently. I love working here, but Nikki is downright heartbroken. It's not natural for a girl that age to cry and mope and pine so much."

She was right, Jake acknowledged morosely, adjusting a foot in the stirrup; it wasn't natural, and he was certain it wasn't healthy. Today's running-away episode had shown him just how serious the situation was. He'd thought the child would get over her attachment to Sarah if she didn't see her on a daily basis, but her feelings seemed stronger than ever. His daughter was clearly miserable, and it was all his fault.

Lack of control—that was what it all boiled down to. He'd intended to shield his child from exactly the sort of emotional pain she was now experiencing, but he'd lost control of the situation with Sarah. He'd let her stay too long, get too close, care too much.

Leaning on the saddle horn, he pinpointed the Big Dipper

in the night sky and wondered if he could similarly pinpoint exactly where he'd gone wrong with Sarah. Was it the night he'd tried to help her see how beautiful she was, and had ended up holding her naked in front of that mirror? No. He'd been head over heels long before that. Was it when he'd first kissed her? No, he'd already been obsessed with her for some time. When he'd first wanted to kiss her? Criminy, that would have been when he'd first seen her in that field.

Straightening in the saddle, he turned the big horse around and headed back down the trail, pressing his heels against the stallion's sides and urging him into a trot. He must have made his big mistake even earlier—probably when he'd decided to saddle up Wildfire and take him out for a ride that afternoon. If he hadn't done that, he wouldn't have been thrown, Sarah wouldn't have come looking for him, and Nikki wouldn't be heartbroken now.

Even in his current black mood, Jake realized the absurdity of his reasoning. He had no control over things like horses being spooked by snakes. But he did have control over his emotions.

Didn't he?

The question pierced him like an arrow, causing him to pull on the reins, yanking the horse to a halt. He'd always thought emotional involvement was a choice. Suddenly he was no longer sure.

Maybe it wasn't just emotional involvement. Maybe it was love.

And maybe it wasn't a matter of choice. Maybe it was like Sarah had said—maybe it just *was*.

The idea rattled through him, shaking him to the core. He couldn't be in love, he argued with himself. He'd avoided that like a bull avoided a bull pen, and with valid reason. He knew from personal experience what the penalty for a failed relationship was—loneliness, despair, a sense of failure, pain. He'd paid the penalty for his father's unhappy marriages, then he'd paid it again in his own. The price was too high to risk another time.

But he was already paying the price, he realized with chagrin. And so was Nikki.

"Hell's bells," he muttered, running a hand down his face and heaving a sigh that felt like it came from the soles of his boots. He might as well face it—despite all of his intentions otherwise, he'd fallen in love with Sarah. And despite his determination not to get involved, he already was.

How had he ended up in this sorry situation? Marriage was the only possible arrangement to offer a woman like Sarah, but he couldn't enter into a marriage knowing the cards were stacked against him. He'd only seen examples of what *not* to do in a marriage. He had no idea how two people were supposed to act behind closed doors in order to have a successful relationship. Could a person exhibit behavior they'd never seen modeled before? He didn't know. He only knew it was a huge emotional risk.

His eyes rested on the shadowed outline of trees across the pasture. He was accustomed to taking other types of risk, of course—that was the nature of ranching. Things like weather and market prices and the health of his herd were all subject to sudden changes, all beyond his control. He'd always accepted the ups and downs of his business, understanding that every drought would eventually end, every bad season would eventually be offset by a good one, every rough spot would sooner or later be replaced by a period of smooth sailing. He'd always taken a long-term view, rationalizing that if he just hung in there, and gave it his best effort, things would all work out in the end.

But marriage was entirely different.

Wasn't it? The question made him stiffen in the saddle.

Maybe it wasn't so different. Maybe he could apply the same principles to a relationship.

His fingers curled around the saddle horn, his pulse quickening, his thoughts racing. Marriage was a risk, true, but risks weren't always negative. With mounting excitement, he recalled surprising turns of good weather, market windfalls, and other wonderful things that had unexpectedly gone his way over the years.

Maybe, just maybe, a romantic involvement wasn't doomed to failure after all. Maybe he wasn't destined to repeat his mistakes as his father had. Maybe he'd learned and grown enough to keep from making those mistakes in the future. Maybe, just maybe, he *was* capable of making and keeping a woman happy, of sustaining a loving, life-long relationship.

An owl soared through the night sky, and his spirits took flight as well. Everything about Sarah was different from Clarissa, especially his feelings. He craved Sarah physically, but he loved a million other things about her—her strength of character, her generous spirit, her warm, kind heart.

If those things were different, didn't it stand to reason that a marriage to Sarah would be different, as well? Not just because of who she was, but because of who he became when he was around her. Sarah had a way of uplifting him, of making him a better person for having been in her presence.

Besides, he had nothing to lose and everything to gain. He and Nikki were both already so in love with Sarah it was killing them to be separated from her. When he looked at it from that perspective, it didn't seem like much of a risk at all.

He turned Wildfire toward the barn, flapped the reins against his flank, and gave him his head. The horse broke into a canter. Jake leaned over his neck, the wind in his face, his heart pounding like the stallion's hooves on the hard dirt trail.

He only hoped Sarah would be willing to take a gamble, too. She'd refused to even come and talk to him tonight. He was afraid he'd hurt her so badly that she'd permanently barricaded him from her heart.

He had to convince her—for Nikki's sake as well as his own. Filled with an urgent sense of purpose, he clenched his jaw determinedly and goaded his horse into a gallop.

Sarah huddled on her living-room sofa, blankly staring at the flickering black-and-white images on her TV screen, too preoccupied with the mental images of a towheaded child and a tall, dark cowboy to appreciate the antics of Laurel and Hardy. She'd rented the old movie to try to cheer herself up, but it wasn't working.

Nothing was working. A bowl of her favorite comfort food, cream-of-potato soup, sat uneaten on the coffee table. She didn't have the appetite or energy to open the half-gallon of double-fudge-ripple ice cream in her freezer. Even donning her most delicate silk nightie, her plushest velour bathrobe and her most expensive perfume had done nothing to lift her spirits.

Deb had called and tried to persuade her to have dinner with her and Harry, but Sarah had wanted to be alone. She wasn't fit company for anyone or anything other than an economy-size box of hankies. Worrying about Nikki today, realizing that the adorable child loved her so much that she was running away to be with her, had shredded Sarah's heart like a used tissue.

And that wasn't even counting what seeing Jake had done to her. When he'd embraced her on that lawn, she'd felt like the sky had parted and heaven had fallen into her lap. Being in his arms, being included in that moment of celebration and love, was like a dream come true.

But it had only been a cruel illusion—a tantalizing glimpse of what she wanted with all her heart, but was destined never to have: a life with Jake and Nikki. Her entire time at the ranch had been like that. It had been a taunting taste of paradise, just enough to ensure she would never be satisfied with anything else.

Just her luck, she thought morosely, curling her feet under her and hunkering down beneath the wool afghan.

She'd irrevocably given her heart to a man who had finally managed to convince her she was lovable, only to discover he stubbornly refused to love her himself.

The doorbell chimed as Sarah dabbed at her eyes. At first she thought it was a sound effect of the movie, but when she glanced at the television, Laurel and Hardy were in the middle of a cornfield. It rang again. Deb must have dropped by to check on her, Sarah thought, dragging herself to the door.

Her heart stopped when she looked through the peephole. *Jake.* She froze, her hand on the doorknob, her knees suddenly as weak as her pulse.

"Sarah, are you there?"

Her fingers were stiff, and it took her a moment to unlock the door.

He stood on the other side of the threshold, tall and somber and impossibly handsome, clutching a bedraggled bunch of chrysanthemum buds. She pulled her forest-green robe tightly across her chest, subconsciously trying to shield her pounding, aching heart.

"I know it's late, but I had to see you." He stepped into the hallway, not waiting to be invited, and closed the door behind him. The temperature of the house suddenly seemed to skyrocket.

Sarah nervously fingered her velour lapel. "Is Nikki having trouble falling asleep again?"

"It took her a while, but she finally conked out."

"Oh." They gazed at each other, the silence deepening until it was almost unbearable.

Jake thrust the flowers at her. "These are for you. I picked them from your and Nikki's garden. I know they're not blooming yet, but maybe they will if you put them in water."

Sarah took the rangy stems, moved that he'd brought her flowers, not having the heart to tell him that it would be another month before chrysanthemums were due to blossom. Trust Jake to look at an ugly stalk and a few knobby buds and see flowers.

Just like he'd looked at her and seen beyond her appearance. Fresh pain, new and acute, stabbed her chest. How ironic, she thought, that his own attractiveness had nearly blinded her to how wonderful he genuinely was.

"The last time you came by, Nikki was needing the princess story," Sarah said, searching for something, anything to fill the silence. "I thought perhaps the tape had broken...."

Jake took a step toward her, invading her personal space. He placed his hands on her shoulders, and the feel of his hands on her body sent a tremor coursing through her.

His eyes were deep and penetrating as they met hers. "Nikki's not the one who needs that story tonight. I am. I especially need the 'happily ever after' part. And I don't want to just hear it, Sarah. I want to live it."

The sound of the movie drifted from the other room, adding a surreal dimension to the moment. Sarah's heart caught in her throat.

"I...I don't understand," she murmured, her heart banging against her rib cage, her breath snagging in her throat. She couldn't bear to be wrong, couldn't stand to read something into his words that wasn't there. If her hopes were raised only to be dashed, it would kill her.

Jake's hands slid down the back of her arms. "I love you, Sarah."

Joy burst through Sarah's veins like fireworks on the Fourth of July. She gazed up at him, her heart skyrocketing.

His dark eyes were full of heartfelt emotion. "I've been fighting the way I feel about you because I didn't want to risk another failed relationship, but living without you is no life at all. I love you and I need you and I want you back in my life."

"Oh, Jake," she murmured, her heart overflowing.

"I've never seen a 'forever' kind of marriage at close range, but that's what I want with you." His gaze poured over her, as warm and sweet as hot fudge. "What I lack in experience, I promise to make up for in effort. I'll do my best to make you happy. If we hit rough times, I promise I'll do whatever it takes to work things out. So what do you say? Will you take a chance and marry me?"

Would she take a chance on getting everything she'd ever wanted in life, and then some? A chance on loving and being loved for the rest of her life by a man who could make her heart stop with a look, her skin burn with a touch, her soul rejoice just by walking into a room—a man who'd peeled the plain brown wrapper off her Plain Jane exterior like a cocoon off a butterfly, who'd shown her all her beautiful colors, who'd taught her how to fly?

"Yes, Jake." She wrapped her arms around his neck and pulled his face down toward her. "Yes, yes, yes!"

Her wholehearted assent was still on her lips as his mouth lowered to hers. And as she closed her eyes and lost herself in the kiss, she could swear she saw fireworks explode across the night sky.

* * * * *

ELIZABETH AUGUST

Continues the twelve-book series—36 HOURS—in November 1997 with Book Five

CINDERELLA STORY

Life was hardly a fairy tale for Nina Lindstrom. Out of work and with an ailing child, the struggling single mom was running low on hope. Then Alex Bennett solved her problems with one convenient proposal: marriage. And though he had made no promises beyond financial security, Nina couldn't help but feel that with a little love, happily-ever-afters really could come true!

For Alex and Nina and *all* the residents of Grand Springs, Colorado, the storm-induced blackout was just the beginning of 36 Hours that changed *everything!* You won't want to miss a single book.

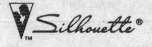

Take 4 bestselling love stories FREE

Plus get a FREE surprise gift!

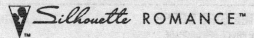

As seen on TV!
Free Gift Offer

With a Free Gift proof-of-purchase from any Silhouette® book,
you can receive a beautiful cubic zirconia pendant.

This gorgeous marquise-shaped stone is a genuine cubic
zirconia—accented by an 18" gold tone necklace.
(Approximate retail value $19.95)

Send for yours today...
compliments of *Silhouette*®

To receive your free gift, a cubic zirconia pendant, send us one original proof-of-purchase, photocopies not accepted, from the back of any Silhouette Romance™, Silhouette Desire®, Silhouette Special Edition®, Silhouette Intimate Moments® or Silhouette Yours Truly™ title available at your favorite retail outlet, together with the Free Gift Certificate, plus a check or money order for $1.65 U.S./$2.15 CAN. (do not send cash) to cover postage and handling, payable to Silhouette Free Gift Offer. We will send you the specified gift. Allow 6 to 8 weeks for delivery. Offer good until December 31, 1997, or while quantities last. Offer valid in the U.S. and Canada only.

Free Gift Certificate

Name: _____

Address: _____

City: _____ State/Province: _____ Zip/Postal Code: _____

Mail this certificate, one proof-of-purchase and a check or money order for postage and handling to: SILHOUETTE FREE GIFT OFFER 1997. In the U.S.: 3010 Walden Avenue, P.O. Box 9077, Buffalo NY 14269-9077. In Canada: P.O. Box 613, Fort Erie, Ontario L2Z 5X3.

FREE GIFT OFFER   084-KFD

ONE PROOF-OF-PURCHASE
To collect your fabulous FREE GIFT, a cubic zirconia pendant, you must include this original proof-of-purchase for each gift with the properly completed Free Gift Certificate.

084-KFDR

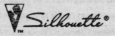